Folk Tales
of the
Night

Stories for Campfires,
Bedtime and Nocturnal
Adventures

Chris Salisbury

Illustrated by Bea Baranowska

Dedication

For Torin, a little boy whose flame flickered so brightly in the endless night, and whose lifeblood was nourished by stories.

Gratitude

For all the colourful threads of tales that have woven the world tapestry of cultures, and to the storytellers who tended the flames of their tradition, so that future generations may prosper in loving stewardship of our sacred Earth.

First published 2023
Reprinted 2024

The History Press
97 St George's Place, Cheltenham,
Gloucestershire, GL50 3QB
www.thehistorypress.co.uk

Text © Chris Salisbury, 2023
Illustrations © Bea Baranowska, 2023

The right of Chris Salisbury to be identified as the Author
of this work has been asserted in accordance with the
Copyright, Designs and Patents Act 1988.

British Library Cataloguing in Publication Data.
A catalogue record for this book is available from the British Library.

ISBN 978 1 80399 039 2

Typesetting and origination by The History Press
Printed and bound in Great Britain by TJ Books Limited, Padstow, Cornwall.

Trees for LYfe

Contents

Here's a companion volume to Chris Salisbury's Wild Nights Out. *These are wonderful stories to tell by firelight or under the stars, drawn from many cultures and exploring the mysteries of the night-time and all it holds. And they're retold by a storyteller who knows just what he's doing, Chris has for many years made traditional tales a key part of his practice as an outdoor educator.*
Hugh Lupton

An enchanting treasury of magical tales handed down through the ages. Infectious and soul-stirring, these are stories crying out to be shared.
Ben Hoare, award-winning wildlife journalist and nature nerd

With Chris Salisbury you are in safe, wise hands. This is the perfect companion to his essential Wild Nights Out, *a glittering selection of tales to honour the collective consciousness of what held us and our ancestors together.*
Ashley Ramsden, founder of the School of Storytelling (UK)

A rich collection about the importance of a dark skies, cycles of the moon, and stories of the stars. These stories come from Chris's long relationship with the natural world and respect for traditional cultures. Enjoy them at bedtime, around the campfire and underneath the stars.
Sally Pomme Clayton

This book honours the richness of the dark hours, drawing together a constellation of stories that language the mystery, wonder, terror and necessity of night. A wonderful resource for any storyteller – the stories call to be spoken aloud in the company of others and the firelight. A vibrant legacy of a life lived in deep apprenticeship and companionship with the wild, Chris has created a guide rich in dreaming and practical knowledge.
Dr Jo Blake, storyteller and theatre-maker

What an absolute gem this book is.
Cotswold Life

Foreword

This is treasure, what you have in your hands. A University of life, all of itself. There's a wily genius throughout these stories that tell us about how to live, to encounter challenge, even to bless. Chris Salisbury's been a storyteller since Noah was a boy (or getting on for thirty years), and I've delighted in his tales in almost every kind of setting: from under a majestic beech at mid-summer to the wires and lights of a modern theatre. The thing that stays unchanged in all these landscapes is the rapt look in the gaze of the listeners. They are off on some kind of magic carpet ride. Don't wait up.

I'm especially pleased there's a section on ghost stories. Chris is the finest teller of ghost stories I've come across. He never hurries but waits till the fire is down to the embers, waits till the candle is casting odd shadows on the cottage wall. Then, maybe, he'll begin. Some of his favourites are in this book. It's always a furtive walk back to the tent after Chris's storytelling. Who knows who's peering in from the woods?

These beautiful stories are a bundle of stars that light up not just the darkness of the night but the darkness within us, within our culture. I would suggest taking one story a week and making it your teacher. They're robust, they have nuance, they have something to tell you. And never hear a story and think it not your duty to pass it on.

Folk Tales of the Night is a book curated by a man that loves his craft. You can feel it within the words and you can trust it. These stories don't just live on his laptop, but out there amongst starlings, curling rivers, winding smoke, and the jubilant look in his kiddie's eyes as they say, again! again!

Martin Shaw
2023

About the Author

Chris Salisbury is a professional storyteller (aka 'Spindle Wayfarer'), who has been telling stories around the campfire and leading night walks for twenty-seven years. He co-founded the Westcountry and Oxford Storytelling Festivals and founded WildWise (www.wildwise.co.uk) in 1999 after many years as education officer for Devon Wildlife Trust. With a background in the theatre, a training in therapy and a career in outdoor education, he uses every creative means at his disposal to encourage people to enjoy and value the natural world on the courses and programmes he runs for WildWise.

He directs the acclaimed 'Call of the Wild' programme for educators-in-training amongst various other courses and events. His first book, *Wild Nights Out: The Magic of Exploring the Outdoors After Dark* (2021), with foreword by Chris Packham, has received excellent reviews.

He is the founder of the Animate School of Narrative Arts, which teaches storytelling skills.

He is married with four children and lives in enchantment in the Dart Valley, Devon.

Introduction

How insupportable would be the days, if the night with its dews and darkness did not come to restore the drooping world.

Henry David Thoreau

Without a second thought, at the day's end, we switch on the lights to continue whatever activity we were pursuing, or simply for sanctuary from the threatening dark. Lest we forget, it wasn't always like this. For most of our history, the night held terrors in the form of apex predators with claws and teeth and we were humbled into submissive mode without the comforting daylight. Then along came the capacity to generate fire, and along with that a chance to keep the darkness, and the animals, at bay while we enjoyed the warmth and companionship of the hearth. Thus, the perfect habitat for stories and storytelling had arrived, and humanity indulged themselves with the oral tradition for thousands of years. Until today, when the practice has sadly subsided, largely succumbing to the proliferation of artificial light.

A particular acceleration point was when our homes were electrified, which afforded us the luxury of extended hours of bright light so the day's activity could continue unabated. However, as well as interfering with our circadian rhythms, so important for the sleep cycle, the advent of artificial light had a dramatic effect on stories and storytelling. More so when that other gear-change development came with the advent of television, and latterly the prevalence of all screen devices. As the old saying goes on the Isle of Lewis, 'When the television came in through the front door, the stories went out the back door.'

The night had always gathered people together, around the warmth and protection of the fire, or the soft atmosphere of lamplight. The shadowy dark was the ideal projection screen for our innate imaginations which, for thousands of years, were indulged by storytelling. The night-time is liminal space, a psychoactive context for us to engage the imaginal realms of the story world. The relatively blank screen of the dark provided the perfect backdrop on which to project the images that flowed forth from the storyteller's mouth. The night-time was story time – and still is for those cultures who live without electricity and screens.

The stories in this book are meant to be spoken aloud, in honour of the great tradition from which they come. Anthologies of oral narratives often seem a little lifeless on the page, and it could be said this strange 'new' literary form of recording them in writing is an act of imprisonment. They deserve instead to be filtered through the living strata of human flesh, bone, breath and memory so they can spring to life again, fresh and revitalised. Tell these stories as a storyteller, and you will be amazed how they seem to have a life of their own. As the old saying goes, 'Read a story and it goes from the eye to the brain, tell a story and it goes from the mouth to the heart'.

Here, I've done my best to make them a pleasure to read too and, by all means, read them aloud to your kids. However, I want to encourage you to learn at least one and see for yourself the difference in the experience, for both you and whoever is listening, and how your life experience and imagination can help the story take flight with new wings.

This anthology is divided into chapter headings that reflect the night's constituency. Thus, there are the obvious components of the night, featuring stories about the moon and stars, but also a procession of dramas and characters that are engendered by the darkness, at least from a human perspective.

As is the storyteller's wont, the repertoire is drawn from a wide variety of sources. This 'pick and mix' process is the artistic licence of the storyteller, who appreciates the nature of the oral tradition. Another aphorism advises, 'When you are telling a story, it's yours. When it is finished, you give it away, as a gift.' In that spirit, despite some sensitivities about colonialism, I offer every story I tell with respect to the genius of the culture from which it came. It's one of the ways culture is shared. In this way, the emphasis is very much on gift-giving, and the sharing of culture, as an enrichment. The underlining principle in this tradition is that because it's not a script, there's no copyright. Authorship is gained by the process of re-presenting the material, which changes it, and is one of the reasons that many stories gain immortality in a constantly evolving and emergent continuum.

Stories are, by their nature, promiscuous, which means they will go anywhere, with anyone. They have always had a certain sort of currency between travellers, merchants and migrants. Tales would have been exchanged and then transplanted in their new habitat, evolved and refreshed by new tellers to take up residency in a new community. Not unlike a virus, really.

And like a virus, they are contagious. It is my hope that these tales will infect you to the degree that you will share them with others, helping them to live again.

CJS – February 2023

One

Origins of
the Night

*Stories of Birth,
Becoming and
Banishment*

Introduction

The night always carries its liminal invitation.

Martin Shaw

Anyone who is a parent or teacher of young children will testify to the sweetness of their curiosity about how the world was made. In the old days, the answer would come in the form of a traditional tale.

Traditional narratives address fundamental questions, and every culture, the world over, has a diaspora of tales to explain the beginning of things. In preliterate cultures and before the Age of Reason had taken insidious root in today's culture, the stories lent themselves to natural phenomena which, once upon a time, didn't have a scientific narrative to explain – for example, the arrival of the darkness or the coming of the light. The stories in this chapter are akin to Creation myths, and for early peoples were the natural habitat for active imaginations that could project onto the blank canvas of the dark.

Without the anchor of reason and rationale, the human imagination is free to speculate, characterise and create narratives that can provide extra dimensions to the phenomenal world, making us relate to and think about things differently. These are those stories that I hope will bring enrichment and wonder to the mysterious night-time realm.

Where Night Came From

Brazil

Once upon a time, in the time before time was measured
by clocks, when the world had just been made, there was
no darkness, because there was no night. It was daytime
all the time. No one had ever seen a sunrise or sunset; the
people knew no starlight or moonlight. In those times,
therefore, there was a complete absence of creatures of
the night, and no night-scented flowers. The only shadows
were those created by the sun, and nobody knew the deep
quiet and stillness of the dark.

In those days, the old stories say, there was a mighty sea
serpent who lived in the depths of the ocean, whose daughter one day married one of the people who lived on the land.
She left her home among the deep, dark depths of the sea
and came to dwell with her husband in the land of the sun.

Her eyes soon grew weary of the bright everlasting
days, and her beauty became bleached and faded. Her
husband watched her with dismay, but he did not know
what to do to help her.

But his new wife knew the medicine she needed was
respite from the fiery heat of the sun, and she craved the
cool dark. 'Oh, if night would only come to this land,' she
moaned as she searched wearily for what shadows she
could find to rest in. 'Here it is always bright, but in my

father's kingdom there are many shadows. Oh, for a little of that darkness!'

'What is this night?' her husband would ask. 'Tell me more about it and perhaps I can find some for you.'

'Night,' she said, 'is the name we give to the heavy shadows which darken my father's kingdom in the depths of the ocean. I love the sunlight of your earth land, but I grow very weary of it. If we could have only a little of the darkness of my father's kingdom to give rest to our eyes, at least for part of the time.'

Her husband at once called his two brothers and asked them to help him on a quest. He explained that they must journey to the kingdom of the sea serpent to bring darkness back for his suffering wife.

The three brothers set forth upon the quest, and after a long and dangerous journey, across thrice nine lands and seven seas, a journey requiring all their strength, skill and cunning, they contrived to arrive at the serpent's kingdom in the depths of the seventh sea, and there they asked him to give them some of the shadows of night to carry back to the earth land for his daughter. The serpent at once obliged and gave them a sack made of the skins of dog-fish, and which had been securely fastened with a binding of bladderwrack. The serpent warned them not to open it until they were once more in the presence of his daughter.

The three brothers thanked the serpent and immediately started out for home, bearing the huge sack of night upon their backs. But as they carried their burden homeward, they began to hear strange sounds within the bag. Sounds they had never heard before. These were the voices of all the night beasts, all the night birds, and all the night insects. They were calling and clamouring and crying out, and at first the three brothers were frightened.

'Perhaps we should drop the bag full of night, and run away as fast as we can,' said the youngest. They set the bag down and retreated to a safe distance, to consider it.

When their fears had subsided, they grew more curious to know what was inside the bag. They heard the beautiful melodic song of the nightingale and wanted to see the musician. The nightjar sounded like some strange mechanical thing, and they wanted to meet the machine that made it. The hoot of the owl was mesmerising, but all together the sounds had a hypnotic effect on them. The more they listened to the wild orchestrations, the more their curiosity grew, until they were desperate to know what the sack contained.

Suddenly, the middle brother stood up and said, 'By my beard, I am going to open the bag and see once and for all what is making this mysterious music!'

And before the others could stop him, he did exactly that. No sooner had he untied it than out rushed the great black cloud of night and riding the tide of darkness that poured forth were all the nocturnal beasts and birds. The brothers screamed and ran as fast as they could, and they didn't stop running until they were home.

The daughter of the sea serpent was waiting anxiously for their return, scanning the horizon every day. One day, she saw what seemed to be a dark cloud of thunder broiling up on the western horizon, but then she saw the three brothers running frantically before it.

As the tide of darkness arrived with the brothers, she cried out, 'At last! Night has come. Night has finally come.' And no sooner had she spoken these words than the cloud of night seemed to perch on her eyelids, and she fell fast asleep.

When she awoke, she felt greatly refreshed. She felt rested and becalmed by the passage of the night. She had dreamt for the first time since she had left the sea. She was once more the happy princess who had left her father's kingdom in the depths of the great seas to come to the earth land. She was now ready for the day again.

She stretched and, as she looked up, she saw a bright shining star hanging low in the eastern sky, and she said, 'Oh, what a beautiful star you are! Henceforth, you shall be called the morning star and you shall be the sun's herald and forewarn of the approach of day. You shall reign and be queen of the sky at this hour every morning.'

Then she called all the birds about her and said to them, 'Oh, wonderful, sweet singing birds, henceforth by my royal decree. I request you to sing your sweetest songs to herald the approach of day.' The nightingale, owl and nightjar were perched in a nearby tree. 'You three shall be appointed the watchmen of the night. Your voices shall be heard in the night and shall warn the others that the day is over. At the end of the night, the other birds will sing to greet the rise of the sun, let this be known as the chorus of the dawn.'

To this very day, those birds still sing in the night-time. And all the other birds sing their sweetest songs in that very first hour of the day, singing up the sun, and this we now call the dawn chorus. And still Venus reigns as the brightest star in the sky.

Basket of Darkness

Kono, Sierra Leone

Long, long ago the Kono people say, the world was bathed in continuous light. There was no darkness. Even when the golden rays of the sun sank beneath the horizon, still the bright silver ribbons of light would be reflected in the Moon.

God wanted to imbue the Earth with another special atmosphere and so created darkness, then put it in a basket to send it up to the Moon to disperse. He chose Bat for the task, as she was such a good flier, and summoned her. Bat was very pleased to be selected and listened carefully as God explained that she was to carry the special basket through the sky all the way to the Moon. Once there, God explained, she was to give it to the Moon and say that God would soon be along to explain how darkness could be used.

Bat lashed the basket to her back and set off on her long journey. After a while, she grew tired and hungry, so she placed the basket down and went to find some food.

In her absence, some animals came by and were curious about what might be in the basket. Of course, they hoped it might be food, and always being hungry, they started to have a closer look. Just as they were prising the lid off the basket, Bat returned and chased them away. But it was too late. The darkness had seeped out and was covering the land.

Bat tried to gather it back, flapping her wings furiously to waft it back in the basket, but to no avail. By the time the sun rose, she was exhausted, and so she slept. When she awoke, the sun was setting, and she took to the skies and again tried to flap the darkness back into the basket, so she could fulfil her task. But it was a hopeless endeavour, and even though she attempts this every night, she never succeeds.

And that is why the faithful bats still, to this very day, fly the way they do at night, flapping their wings as fast as they can to waft the darkness back into the basket.

Crow Brings Daylight

Inuit, Alaska

A long time ago, when the world was first born, it was always dark in the north country where the Inuit people lived, and where it was covered with snow for 300 days a year. They presumed that darkness covered the world until Crow told them about daylight and how he had seen it sometimes on his long journeys. The more they heard about daylight, the more the people grew curious, and the more curious they got, the more they wanted it. The more they wanted it, the more they considered it.

'If there was daylight, we could hunt further and for longer,' they said. 'We could see the polar bears coming and run before they attack us.'

The people begged Crow to go and bring them daylight, but he didn't want to. 'It's a long way and I'm too old to fly that far,' he said.

But the people did not relent in their request, and they begged until he finally agreed to go. He flapped his coal-black wings and launched into the dark sky, towards the east. He flew for a long time until his wings were aching. He was about to turn back when he saw the dim glow of daylight in the distance. 'At last, there is the daylight,' said the tired Crow.

As he flew towards the dim light it became brighter and brighter until the whole sky was in bright light, and he could see for miles. The exhausted bird landed in a tree near a village to rest. It was very cold. He rested and watched.

Soon, his beady eye saw the daughter of the village chief coming to the river. She dipped her bucket in the icy water and returned to her father's snow lodge. Crow followed and perched outside the entrance to glean what he could.

Inside the snow lodge it was warm and bright, and Crow saw the chief's grandson playing on the lodge floor. After a while he started to cry.

'What's the matter? Why are you crying?' asked the chief, who was sitting at the fire. The chief wanted his favourite grandson to be happy and told his daughter to fetch the box of daylight balls.

When she returned, she opened the box and took out a small ball of daylight, which glowed like a small sun. She wrapped a string around it and gave it to her son to play with. The child stopped crying and played with the ball, rolling it around the lodge until it rolled out of the entrance and into the snow, where Crow was waiting.

Quick as a flash, Crow put out his talon, grasped the string on the ball of daylight and flew up into the sky, heading west, flying as fast as he could.

Eventually, he reached the land of the Inuit people again and, in his exhaustion, he let go of the string. The ball of daylight dropped to the ground and shattered into tiny pieces. Light streamed everywhere, and the darkness left the sky.

All the people came from their lodges. 'This is a great wonder! Look how far we can see! Look how blue the sky is, and the mountains in the distance!' They were filled with so much joy and wonder and thanked Crow for bringing the daylight to their land.

'This one ball of daylight will need to gain its strength from time to time. So, you'll only have daylight for half the year.'

The people replied, 'But we're happy to have daylight for half the year! Before you brought the ball to us it was dark all the time!'

And so that is why, in the land of the Inuit peoples, in the far north, it is dark for one half of the year and light for the other half. The people never forgot it was Crow who brought them the gift of daylight and they take care never to hurt him – in case he decides to take it back.

Darkness Versus Daylight

In the beginning, there was only darkness.

From the shadows came the creatures and in those times of long ago there was no difference between animals and people, and they shared the same language. In those ancient times, there was an understanding that the words they spoke had power and magic and were like spells that could be cast to bring about form and feature.

One night, a fox and a hare were having an argument. The fox was using the word 'Darkness!' because he liked the way he could use the cover of the dark to hunt and scavenge food from everyone. The hare, on the other hand, kept repeating the word 'Daylight!' because she needed light to help her forage for food and to see her predators. The argument went back and forth, and their cries rang out over the hills and hollows– 'Darkness!', 'Daylight!', 'Darkness!', 'Daylight!', 'Darkness!', 'Daylight!' – until such time that a bright, burning light rose over the mountains causing the darkness to shrink back, scuttling away and retreating from the sun, to dwell wherever it could find refuge in the form of shadows.

The word repeated by the hare had had a stronger magic than the fox's word, and fox slipped away to find shade and shadows. But later that day, late in the afternoon, the fox and hare bumped into each other again and they renewed their argument – 'Darkness!', 'Daylight!',

'Darkness!', 'Daylight!', 'Darkness!', 'Daylight!' – until suddenly, the golden light disappeared below the horizon, and now it seemed that fox's word had a stronger magic, for the rising tide of darkness swept over the land, and the land became a realm of the night.

Ever since then, day and night take turns to either shine brightly over the land or cover her over with a dark blanket. The fox and hare also take turns finding their food, but the fox is still cross with the hare and chases her whensoever he sees her, but the hare is always too quick – as long as she can see by the light of day.

The Balance of
Day and Night

Caddo Nation, Arkansas, America

In the beginning, the old people say, the first people had
to live in a world covered in darkness. This was the way it
was, and the people supposed this was the way it would
always be. They survived by hunting the black deer, and
gathering different plants and roots, and they even appre-
ciated all the blessings of living under a blanket of night.

Coyote, however, was not so sure, and kept asking questions of the people. 'Why is it always dark?', he would say.
'Why shouldn't there be more light to see by?'

His restless, enquiring mind would not relent, and, in
the end, the people turned to the wisest woman to see if
she knew how to obtain light. That old medicine woman
gathered and ingested some plants to help her see more
clearly, then she lit a fire in her lodge, and she shook her
snake-skin rattle and sang some medicine songs.

In the morning she came to the council with an answer.
'I journeyed with the deer people, and in my dream, there
were five deer. Each of these deer were different, and
each had a different purpose. There are yellow ones, white
ones, black ones, and spotted and half-spotted ones that
roam all over the Earth. They told me, that if you kill the
yellow deer, everything shall be yellow all the time. If you
kill the white deer, everything shall be white all the time.

If you kill either of the spotted ones, everything shall be spotted and not go well for us. If you kill the black one, everything shall be black, just as it is now. But if you kill both the black and the white deer, then we shall have day as well as night. During the day, everything will be white, bright and light, and we can hunt and gather, and see our children's shining faces. And then when the night comes, it will be dark so we can return to our homes and take refuge and rest.'

The people accepted this and began to hunt both the black and white deer. Sure enough, just as the prophecy had foretold, the daylight arrived, and since that time, the people have enjoyed a balance between day and night.

The Banquet of Strange Delights

Japan

In the beginning of the beginning, when the first gods created the world, they imagined three deities into being: the sun goddess, Amaterasu, the moon god, Tsukuyomi and a god, Susanoo, to rule over the waters of the Earth.

Amaterasu was a supremely creative deity, and wove many gifts for the Earthly realm, including rice and wheat fields, and even brought forth the silkworm so the people could weave cloth. Susanoo, however, was disgruntled and felt short-changed by what he had received. To spite his father, Izanagi, he spurned his domain, and declared allegiance to his mother in the realm of the dead. Izanagi was furious and banished him from Tagamagahara, the shimmering residence of the gods.

Susanoo took refuge with his mother, in the under-world, and there his bitterness took root, especially over his sister's privileges. The jealous storm-god invited himself to the palace of the gods and started throwing his weight around, and in the process, he destroyed much of what his sister had created, including the rice fields. Violent storms erupted with his moods but, despite his behaviour, the gods remained quiet.

Amaterasu was furious with the gods for their reticence in punishing Susanoo, and at the petulance of her brother, so she locked herself away in a cave and sealed the entrance with a great rock. Her retreat took all the light from the world, and the Earth was plunged into a permanent darkness.

This age of darkness caused the world to fall into anarchy and chaos until, at last, the gods intervened. However, Amaterasu still refused to emerge from her refuge. The gods were nonplussed about what to do, until Omoikane, the god of cunning, proposed they hold a banquet outside the cave, and the banquet should be raucous and wild and full of strange delights. There should be jesters, jugglers and plate-spinners, and acrobats, musicians, conjurers and contortionists. Basically, anything and everything to potentially arouse the curiosity of the sun goddess, to coax her out from her cave.

The gods were pleased with this idea. It would, after all, serve their own appetites and delights. The banquet was prepared, produce was piled high upon the table, the troops of entertainers and musicians began to make a festival of strange delights, and the gods kept one eye on the great stone covering the mouth of the cave.

It did not take too long to catch the attention of Amaterasu, who shouted out from her hiding place, 'What in all the gods' names, is going on out there?'

Uzume, the goddess of mirth, sang back to her that they had found a divinity even more beautiful than her, and she should see for herself to believe it. Amaterasu was intrigued by this, and her vanity was provoked. She rolled back the stone and was greeted by the wriggling, jiggling, dancing Uzume, whose preposterous contortions were so bizarre that Amaterasu was captivated, and she couldn't help herself but laugh. And she laughed and laughed, and all the while she was laughing and being distracted in this way, the gods sealed the entrance of the cave by means of a sacred rope.

By the end of the banquet, the mood of Amaterasu had lifted, and she was agreeable to returning to live with the gods again, but only on the condition that her mischievous brother was punished.

And so, it came to be. His beard was cut off, his fingernails and toenails were torn off, and he was expelled from heaven, and they say that was enough to mend his wicked ways. But no doubt there are storytellers who might tell you a different tale!

King of the Birds

They say that if you travel far enough backwards in time, there were so many birds in the sky that no light from the sun reached the ground and the people had to live in shadows. This was a difficult time for the people who lived then, for they were more easily hunted by predators who had the advantage over them in the dark.

At this time, there were two brothers called Lae and Kuat, who were fed up with this situation. No matter how many birds they shot down from the sky, there were always more to take their place.

At length, they decided to take the matter to Urubutsin, the King of the Birds, to make representation on behalf of the people, to see if he was amenable to sharing some of the daylight. They travelled to his kingdom at the edge of the forest, and there they begged Urubutsin to yield to their request. But it was all to no avail, so the brothers went away disheartened, but determined to find a way.

They sat down to think. They needed to come up with a plan. If the King of the Birds was not going to give freely what they wanted, then they were going to have to resort to an ambush. But how to trick the King of the Birds into coming close enough to catch him? There was only one way, they decided, and this was to take advantage of his fondness for carrion – meat from the carcass of a dead animal.

The brothers found a large dead Tapir and hid inside to wait. Before long, Urubutsin flew down to eat and Kuat grabbed his leg and refused to let go until Urubutsin agreed to make a deal.

The deal they struck was that the birds would let in the light of day, and by night the Moon would help the people navigate the darkness. The two brothers returned to the gratitude of their people. Ever since that time, Lae and Kuat have been remembered as the two brothers, the Moon and the Sun.

Two

Moon
Stories

Introduction

*Sing Muses, with your sweet voices. Sing, daughters of Zeus,
son of Kronos. Sing us the story of the long-winged Moon.*

Homer

Without the Moon, would there even be a 'Once upon a
time …'?

It's only a slightly flippant question that is borne
from our long apprenticeship to the moon's cycles. Since
human cultures began flourishing on Earth, the Moon
was relied on as calendar, clock and compass. Its monthly
appearance and disappearance could be used to chart
the progress of time, where other cycles like that of the
sun, for example, were less obvious. And its symbolic and
repetitive enactment of death and rebirth was a celestial
affirmation of what takes place down on Earth, with a
helpful reminder that even when there seems to be an
ending, renewal will surely follow.

And so, these stories offer a handrail to make our way
across troubled ground. They echo the Moon with their
emergence out of the dark, the journey they travel, and
the completion or ending. There is an old understanding
that endings are really only 'tail-ends', before the cycle/
story begins again. It must have been reassuring for our
ancestors to bear witness to this constant renewal played
out by the lunar cycle.

Without exception, the Moon has been held in awe and reverence by human cultures, and not surprisingly, features as subject or protagonist in so many of their tales. Characterised as either male or female, good or bad, the Moon's dual aspect of constancy and change always inspires intrigue and mystery and, for our ancestors, provided a fixed point in a 'faraway realm' on which to conjecture and speculate and dream. Here is some of their dreaming …

The Giant and the Moons

Aboriginal Australia

Beyond the horizon, further than you can see, further than you could even travel and where no one has ever been, is a beautiful land of tree-clad hills, rivers of sparkling clear water and grassy valleys with flowers like cups of honey.

The inhabitants of that land are big, round, shining moon-people, who have no need of legs and arms, but roll about and over the grasses, and they are content because they have everything they need in that sweet realm.

But, from time to time, and usually about once a month and always at night, one of the moon-people will grow restless and an urge will develop to explore beyond what they know, a longing to travel across the vast empty and dark sky-lands. And so, one of the moon-people will suddenly disappear, and everyone knows they will have gone on that long journey.

What they don't know, however, is that just outside the valley lives a huge fire-giant. This fire-giant is too bright even to behold. When this giant sees a moon come wandering, he captures it, and with his flint knife he cuts a slice. Every night he cuts another slice, and another, until he has a pile of shining slices at his feet, like silver apples, and this is all that's left of the big, round moon. The fire-giant cuts up all the slices into tiny pieces and then tidies up, flinging them all over the sky.

These tiny cut-up moons are now terrified of the fire-giant, and so when the Sun emerges at dawn, they hide. All day, they avoid being seen as the Sun marches across the sky. Finally, as the Sun begins to set, they come out from hiding, and little fragments of the moons sparkle with light in the night sky. We know them as stars, and that's why they only come out at night.

Don't Curse the Moon!

Māori, New Zealand

Once upon a time, in the land of the long white cloud, there was a village, and in this village there lived an adolescent girl, and her name was Rona. Rona was prone to moods, especially in this stage of her life, and she was already feeling grumpy when her mother asked her to fetch water from the nearby river.

Rona took the gourd and sullenly left to do as she was asked. But the night has no sympathy for moodiness, and when the girl tripped over a tree root, stubbing her toes, she cursed the moon for being behind a cloud and not lighting her way.

Curse a deity at your peril!

The moon goddess heard this stream of abuse and was affronted. She snatched the girl to take her up into the sky as punishment, but Rona grabbed hold of the branches of the ngaio tree and would not let go, issuing forth a stream of obscenities.

There was a struggle then. Goddess and girl hefted and heaved until finally the moon goddess prised her away and carried her into the night sky. Rona, however, had clung onto those branches and uprooted the whole tree, which then travelled with her as she was placed in confinement inside the moon palace.

When you look up at a full moon, you see a woman still holding that ngaio tree and her gourd.

The story reminds us to be careful not to insult the moon, or any of the deities and denizens of the night!

The Blacksmith and the Moon

Mandingo, Africa

We suppose that everything around us has always been the way that it is. And that's a fair assumption when it comes to celestial skies.

But suppose it wasn't. Suppose things came to be because of certain people and certain events, in time and space.

Well, the story is told in the Mandingo tradition that for the first people, there was no moon at night, and they tell of how it got hung up high in the sky.

They say that life for those people was very much the same. They played and worked hard, they raised families, they grew sick or old. But in those times, there was no visit from Death. Instead, whenever the moment came, be it weariness, old age or sickness, they simply walked away towards an old iron chain that hung down from the sky and climbed up to begin their next life in the other world.

This story begins with a blacksmith called Fazog Bo Si, who had worked himself to the bone over many years, slaving away on a hot forge, hauling lumps of iron and bags of coal. He had no apprentices or sons, and his three daughters, although they loved their father, had no intentions to learn his trade.

So it was that his head and shoulders began to sag under the burden of work, and after years of sweat and toil over the roaring hot forge, he felt his time had come. At length, in the middle of pounding a big piece of iron, he simply stopped, turned and walked away from the forge for the last time. He hadn't even bothered to put down the iron he was heating.

He walked until he came to the iron chain hanging down from the sky, and then, still holding the piece of iron, he climbed. As it happened, his daughters saw him climbing, and they wept for him, and for the loss of their father. The eldest daughter then said to the others, 'I can't bear it! Let's follow him up the chain, and then, when we are at the top, let's pull up that stupid chain, and then at least nobody else will ever be able to follow, and no one will lose their father or mother again!'

And this is exactly what they did. They climbed to the top, and then they hauled up that heavy iron chain. Who knows what they saw up there, or if they were reunited with their father, or what the skylands of the Otherworld were like. What we do know is that in the absence of the chain, death came among the people, as we know it today.

The piece of iron that Fazog Bo Si held was still hot from the forge, and he hung it up in the sky and it became the moon. The Mandingo people say that when the moon rises red on the horizon, it is the residual red heat from that hot forge of his. Some say that his daughters, and all the ancestors that climbed the chain, are the stars shining brightly in the night sky.

Quadjac and the Man in the Moon

Inuit, Greenland

There was once an orphan boy called Quadjac, who lived in the far north, where it snows and snows, and all the trees are like Christmas trees. He had no family, no home and nobody to protect him. He was barely tolerated by the villagers, and he survived off scraps of walrus hide that were tossed to the dogs. The only one who took pity on him was a young girl who smuggled out items of clothing to keep his thin body warm.

When the people gathered in the singing house, the boy would hover around the doorway, peeping in at the warmth of the fire, listening to the songs and longing to be invited in. Sometimes this happened, but only by being grabbed and lifted by his ears and told to fetch water. This happened so often that his ears stretched and the boys in the village would tease him for his big ears and for his weakness and did not let him join in with their games.

So, you can see, it was a miserable life for Quadjac.

At last, the Moon-Man noticed the plight of Quadjac. It was his sacred duty to protect the orphans, and so he harnessed his silvery, dappled husky dog to his sledge and he drove down to the village one night to help the boy.

He called out to Quadjac, but the boy thought it was one of the men coming to scold him, and so he hid in the shadows.

The Moon-Man called again, and the boy noticed his voice was soft and different from the voices of the men, and he peeped out. He was frightened to see the huge, resplendent form of the Moon-Man, and shrank back.

'I will not hurt you,' said the Moon-Man, 'I am here to help you.' The Moon-Man took the boy's hand, and led him to a flat rock, where he told him to lie down and not be afraid.

Quadjac was afraid, but he dared not disobey. He lay on the rock, under the starry sky, and shut his eyes, afraid of what might happen next.

The Moon-Man took a long, thin moonbeam of light and he began to whip the boy with it. Quadjac felt the rays of silver light as soft strokes on his skin. After several lashes, the Moon-Man called out, 'Do you feel stronger yet?'

'Yes, I do,' said the boy, and it was true, he felt himself grow stronger with each stroke of the moonbeam.

'Now, get up and see if you can lift this rock,' said the Moon-Man.

Quadjac did as he was asked but could not lift the rock. 'It is too heavy,' he said.

'Lie down again,' said the Moon-Man, and he lashed the boy with more strokes. 'Try again,' he said, but again the rock was too heavy for Quadjac.

More strokes followed and, for a third time, Quadjac was told to lift the rock, but this time, he was successful. In fact, he was astonished at how easily he could do it, lifting the heavy rock like it was a small pebble.

'That will do for now,' said the Moon-Man. Tomorrow morning, I shall send three bears. Then you can test your strength to show what power you have.'

The Moon-Man got into his sledge and drove back to his Moon home.

Quadjac watched the shining sled climb into the sky and fade from view. He brought his attention to the new feeling in his body. He had grown in stature as well as strength. He was now a good-sized man rather than a skinny youth.

In the morning he waited for the bears, looking forward to the trial. Three bears did come, growling and looking so fierce that the men of the village ran into their huts and shut the doors. But Quadjac was ready and ran down to the ice field where the bears were.

The men peered out through the window holes, scarcely believing their eyes. 'Can that really be Quadjac?' they said. 'The bears will soon eat the foolish fellow!'

But he seized the first one by its hind legs and threw it like a bowling ball over the ice. The second bear followed the first, slithering and spinning on the ice. But the third bear, he simply picked up and carried up to the village. There, he shouted for everyone to hear, 'See me now! All of you who abused and mistreated me, look who I am now!'

And they did see him, and the years of abuse and neglect ended that day. And the girl who had shown him kindness became his wife.

The Jilted Moon

Chukchee, Siberia

The Moon always travelled alone through the night sky. This was how it was. This was how it had always been. But when he saw the people gathered together, he suddenly felt his loneliness. He was curious to know more and so the Moon took a human form, and moved across the land, studying at close quarters the ways of the people.

One day, he happened upon a wandering herd of reindeer led by a beautiful maiden. Every winter, the reindeer herder sent his daughter to lead his huge herd far away from their home, deep in the snowy land, where they could feed on the pastures. As the maiden and her reindeer travelled, she played upon her flute to entertain herself and the herd to fill the long, dark days.

Travelling across the dark sky, the Moon had heard the maiden's melodies before. Now, hearing this familiar music on the ground, he was lured closer, and before long he was following the reindeer maiden.

He watched her every movement and gazed at her lovely face. Listening to her wistful tunes, he knew he could not live without her. He knew he must marry her and take her home to the sky. This way, he would never be lonely again. And so, he hurried after her, resolving to capture her.

There was one old reindeer who was the protector of the herd, and he sensed the Moon's presence growing closer.

He whispered to the maiden, 'The Moon is near! He wishes to capture you, so we must take care.'

At that moment, the maiden also felt the Moon's presence. 'What shall I do?' she whispered, for she had no desire at all to be captured – not by the Moon or anyone. She loved her life with the herd, and this chase frightened her.

So, the old reindeer buried the maiden under a snowdrift to disguise her. When the Moon reached the herd, he looked around and asked the reindeer, 'Where has your maiden gone?' But the herd ignored him and moved on, trampling the snow underfoot, careful not to step upon the maiden.

As soon as the old reindeer saw that the Moon was lost among the herd, he brought the maiden out, and together they dashed toward the sturdy *yaranga*, the tent where the maiden slept at night.

Meanwhile, the Moon continued searching through the great herd of reindeer, and then saw a light coming from the tent. 'She is there,' he said, and he rushed toward the tent. But just before he reached the door flap, the old reindeer used some old magic to transform her into an oil lamp.

'My love! I've found you,' the Moon called out in excitement as he rushed inside, but when he saw nothing but a bed and the tent poles, a block and a hammer, and in one corner a shining oil lamp, he was mystified. 'Where are you?' he called to the maiden. He listened, but he heard only the steady breathing of the reindeer herd outside the tent.

'Please come to me,' the Moon called, but no one answered him, and so he walked outside the tent and began to search through the herd again. The moment he was gone, the maiden was transformed once more into her own body, and now sensing she could always hide from danger, she opened the tent flap and cried out, 'What's wrong with you? I'm right here!'

Hearing her voice, the Moon raced back toward the yaranga, but before he could reach it, the girl again turned into an oil lamp.

The Moon was frantic. 'Where are you? I hear only your voice,' and again nobody answered.

And so again the Moon walked among the milling reindeer, but once more the girl became herself again and taunted him. 'What is wrong with you? Can you not see me?'

Each time the Moon tried to find her, the girl changed shape, and in this way, she stayed hidden. The Moon became more and more vexed. He rushed this way and that. He cried out, 'Please let me see you!' In his desperate search, he soon became exhausted.

Peeping out of the tent, the girl saw that he was now weakened and tired. She grabbed a sack, ran out of the tent and threw the sack over the Moon's head. Then she bound his legs and arms and pulled him inside her tent.

'Now I have captured *you*!' she said to the Moon.

'Please set me free,' the Moon begged her.

'Why should I? What will you offer me in return?'

Now the Moon had to think carefully. Trapped inside that tent, unable to move at all, he suddenly longed for the freedom of the sky and to return to his own realm. So, at last, he said, 'I promise if you set me free, I shall return to my home. I will offer your people my light during the night, and when they wish for darkness, I shall disappear.

I shall measure out the year, season by season, so that each month has a different light, and there will be times for hunting and times for frost, times for new leaves and new calves and new days.'

'It's a good offer but I cannot let you go,' said the reindeer maiden. 'You will only grow strong again and return to capture me.'

'I will never return,' the Moon said. 'You have my word. Even though my heart is broken, I promise I will help look after your people in this way.'

And so, the reindeer maiden did set the Moon free, and he did return to the sky. Ever since that day, he has cast his light upon the Earth, though sometimes, when he remembers his visit to the land below and his love for the reindeer maiden, his heart grows faint and his light fades. And then everyone knows the Moon is dreaming of his love for the reindeer maiden.

The Moon Maiden

Once there lived a bamboo cutter called Také Tori. He was an older man, very poor and honest and hard-working, and he lived with his wife in a hut on top of a hill, looking down over the bamboo forests. They had no children, which was a cause of sorrow for them as they longed to be parents.

The story begins at the end of one day's cutting, as the sun began to slip below the horizon. Také Tori was about to turn for home when, looking down, he saw something glowing among the green stems of the bamboos. It was an eerie greenish light, pulsing and reaching out to his curiosity.

He pushed his way through the bamboo thicket to get closer to the light but was puzzled to find it obscured. No matter how hard he looked, the source of the light seemed to evade being found. 'Could it be,' he mused aloud, 'that it's inside the bamboo?'

He was determined to find it, and so he began cutting at the thick stem of the biggest bamboo, and the more he cut, the brighter the light grew, until the bamboo fell and there it lay in the hollow stem a shining green jewel.

'Wonder of wonders!' cried Také Tori. 'For five-and-thirty years I've cut bamboo, and in all that time I've never seen the like.' With that, he picked up the jewel, and as soon as it lay in his hands it began to change shape and it became a tiny being, two-legged and fully formed, like a beautiful little fairy, dressed all in green silks.

As he stared in astonishment, the little being greeted him by name, and announced her intention to come and live with him. 'As you wish,' said Také Tori, 'but please understand we are very poor. What we have we will gladly share. Stay as long as you like.'

He hurried home and showed his wife the shining thing in his hands; she could hardly believe her eyes.

In the following days, the fairy grew so fast it was a wonder, and within a few days she had grown to become a fine, tall maiden, as fair as the sparkle of sunlight on stream and as wise and deep as the night. They called her their 'Emerald' as she had come from the shining jewel. But still the mystery remained as to where she had come from, and why.

The husband and wife were overjoyed to have the delightful presence of the maiden, and they fussed over her as if she was their own daughter. For three years they lived in joy, but as the third year turned toward its end, she grew very sorrowful, though she wouldn't say why. She took to sitting at night and gazing at all the phases of the moon, staring intently until it had set.

One evening, the husband and wife were sitting with her as a full moon rose over the eastern horizon. The rolling mists over the hills were glistening in the moonlight, and it was one of those mysterious atmospheres. Adding to the enchantment, the swirling mist seemed to be moving down from the moon.

Také Tori gazed upon the face of Emerald and thought how like the moon she was in her pale and wan beauty, when he noticed a single tear falling down her cheek.

'Whatever is the matter, my sweetness?' asked Také Tori in dismay, for it troubled him so deeply to see their foster daughter in distress.

'This is a sad night,' said Emerald. 'For you see that mist descending? That is the silver road bearing the cohorts of the Moon King. And along the highway come countless celestial forms to bear me home. My father is the King of the Moon. I disobeyed his behest. He sent me into exile for these three years as punishment, and now calls me home.'

Down they came in their myriad forms, bearing tiny, flickering torches of green flame. Silently they came, alighting all around where they sat on top of the hill, now adorned with the silver mist.

'Must you leave us?' said Také Tori, tears now filling his eyes.

'I must. Farewell, Také Tori,' she said, 'and farewell, dear foster mother, and thank you for all your kindness and care. Don't forget me. Let the moon remind you of where I dwell and know that I will look down upon you from my lunar kingdom.'

And then, as silently as they came, the cohort of lights floated away on the mist, bearing the maiden until the husband and wife were left there in the cold night, staring up at the moon, and wondering if it had all been a dream.

A Gift from the Moon

When Yasí, the moon goddess, looked down upon the luscious green mantle covering the Earth, her curiosity grew and she longed to see what was underneath the thick canopy of jungle. She could hear the wild orchestrations of the creatures, and she wanted to see them, and to walk on the soft earth among the plants, flowers and trees.

In the end, she could bear it no longer and persuaded her friend Araí, the cloud goddess, to go with her. Together, they went to ask permission from Kuaray, the Sun, but he was reluctant to let them go for he could not protect them down there. His worry was that on Earth they would be vulnerable to the dangers of the jungle, like any human.

But Yasí and Araí were determined and, in the end, Kuaray gave his blessing, and they travelled down a silver ladder one night and began to explore. They couldn't believe how beautiful the jungle was, and they had so much to look at as they stole quietly between the trees. It was a feast for the eyes!

So absorbed in this new world were both goddesses that they did not notice the jaguar that was following them closely. Jaguar hunted at night and was a master of stealth and silence. Just as the cat was about to pounce, an arrow flew out of nowhere, striking the jaguar on his rump, and so startled was he that he vanished into the night to lick his wound.

The goddesses looked around to see who had fired the arrow, and saw a hunter emerge from the shadows. This was a Guarani hunter, a native of the jungle. He introduced himself and offered to escort them to his hut by the river where he lived with his wife and his daughter. When they arrived, the hunter threw an *acutí* (a rodent) on the fire and offered the meat to his visitors. He also offered them *tambú* (a white-fleshed worm bred in the trunks of the pindó palm tree).

When his wife went to prepare a place for them to sleep, the hunter told the goddesses that they had decided to live alone in the bush to preserve the virtues that Tupá, the god of goodness, had given to their daughter.

They spent a comfortable night, and the next morning, Yasí and Araí sincerely thanked the family for their hospitality and returned home to their celestial refuge.

Yasí could not forget her adventure on Earth. Every night she saw the hunter and his family, remembering his bravery and generosity, and she wanted to give them a special gift. One new moon night, Yasí sprinkled some magic seeds around their hut and asked Araí to rain on them so they would germinate. In the early morning, the hunter and his family were amazed to see some bushes with dark green leaves and small white flowers around their hut.

That same night, Yasí appeared to them in a dream with the following words, 'I am Yasí, the moon goddess. I have left you a gift in gratitude; a plant that you will call *caá* [herb], which will help you to never feel alone. You will share it with all the people of your tribe and offer it to your guests. It will be a symbol of friendship and hospitality. I will bless your daughter with immortality, and she will be the protector deity of this plant. She will now be known as "Caá Yarí", she will live forever and will never lose the innocence, kindness and beauty that she received as a gift from Tupá.'

The moon goddess then showed them how to dry and grind the leaves. She put them inside a *matí* (a hollow gourd), added hot water and, with a reed, sipped the drink. 'The water must not boil, otherwise the infusion will lose its magic,' said Yasí.

The *matí* was passed from hand to hand, refilled when it was empty, and the tea was drunk and enjoyed by everyone. From that time to this, Caá Yarí has walked among the plants, whispering to them and watching over their growth with her grace and protection.

That is how the *yerba mate* plant came to the people of the earth. A beautiful gift from the Moon.

Three

Star
Stories

Introduction

*I is sometimes hearing far away music
coming from the stars in the sky.*

Big Friendly Giant in Roald Dahl's *The BFG*

Whenever I stand in awe under a canopy of stars, I have the sense that our ancestors must have shared the same experience of wonder and perspective that the faraway mysterious cosmos affords us. It feels strangely connecting to past people I never knew, past people who had no technology to unravel some of those secrets as we do today, although thankfully so much of the universe remains a beguiling mystery.

What they did have, however, was the blessing of time to ponder and muse, and what flowed forth from their imaginations were stellar narratives to fill in the blanks in actual knowledge. That's not to underestimate the detailed knowledge that past civilisations acquired through long-term pattern recognition, plotting the movement of the stars and planets to be able to predict cosmic events and the year's turning.

For them, and us, simple stargazing is child's play, a 'join-the-dots' approach – that very satisfying process we all did in our puzzle books as children. This joining of the dots, or stars, made figurative pictures for our ancestors, and when you joined the pictures together what could then follow were narratives of picture sequences.

These stories, to varying degrees, helped to explain cosmic events and patterns of celestial movements and, of course, deepened our acquaintance with the firmament as a whole.

As we know, stories make or deepen relationships to things so that they will be remembered. One of the ways they achieve this is by animating the inanimate, or characterising things to give them agency and life force – much the way you see small children doing with their toys and even everyday objects.

A tiny fraction of the countless narratives from diverse cultures follows. No doubt you've heard that there are more stars in the universe than grains of sand. Here are just a few grains of sand in the form of traditional tales to help connect to the cosmos and remind us of the vastness of the human imagination.

A Necklace of Stars

Philippines

When the world was made, the sky was very close to the ground, and was textured like a rockface, like coral at the bottom of the ocean.

One day, a woman of the first peoples went out to pound rice. She took her big wooden pounding stick to the pounding stone, and before she began, she took off the beads from around her neck lest they got in the way. It was precious to her. So many little white beads had been threaded to make this necklace, and some of them had been painted in bright colours of the rainbow. She took the white bone comb from her hair and hung them both on the sky-roof above.

Then she began to sing. This song was a working song, and helped to pass the time as she pounded the rice.

'Up and down to pound the grain,
from heaven to earth and back again!'

So intent was she in her work that she did not notice that every time she raised her pestle-stick, it struck the sky-roof, and each time it pushed it further away. Then, she raised the pestle so high that it struck the sky very hard, and this time the whole sky-roof began to rise of its own accord, and kept moving up and away, higher and higher. It went so far that the woman lost her necklace and comb.

They were lost into the mysteries of the sky, and the people now say that the white bone comb became the moon and the beads are the stars that are now scattered about the night sky.

Road of Stars

Long, long ago, there was only darkness at night, there was nothing to see when you looked up into the sky.

The people learned, in time, to make fires to light up the darkness and they gathered around these fires to tell the stories of the day and to be together. This was how it was for a long time.

But one night a girl, who sat warming herself by the fire, played with the ashes at the edge. She took the ashes in her hands and threw them up and saw how pretty they were when they floated in the air. She put green sticks from the bushes on the fire and then she stirred the fire with a stick. Bright sparks flew out and up and went high, mixing with the silver ashes. She watched them hanging and flowing together to make a glittering bright road across the dark sky. The people in those times called it the 'Road of Stars'.

The girl was pleased and clapped her hands and danced and began singing:

'The little stars! The tiny stars!
They make a road for other stars.
Ash of wood-fire! Dust of the Sun!
They call the Dawn when Night is done!'

Then she took some of the roots she had been eating and threw them into the sky, to see what would happen to them. They hung there and twinkled. Some types of root turned into flickering stars that gave a red light, others gave a green light, and some gave a golden light. The girl heard them singing while they sparkled:

'We are children of the Sun!
It's so! It's so! It's so!
Him we call when Night is done.
It's so! It's so! It's so!
Bright we sail across the sky,
By the Road of Stars, so high.
We are twinkling, smiling at you,
As we sail our way across the blue.
It's so! It's so! It's so!'

Every night the people came together around their fires, and they gazed up into the wondrous night sky and traced the patterns of movement. They imagined shapes and constellations and watched celestial events unfolding, and they shared the stories around the fire. They saw stars rise and fall and understood that this was a message from the stars telling them of the birth of someone, and whenever a star fell, they knew that someone had died. They watched the night sky continuously for a greater understanding of the sacred dance of life.

How the Pleiades Became

What's in a name? They used to say that names had power and potency, that names were like spells, and if you could decipher the true meaning of the name you were given at birth, it would set you on the path to finding your destiny.

Curious then, that in this story, a man with six sons decided to refer to them in terms of their ages. Hence, they were called the Oldest, the Next to the Oldest, the Next to the Next to the Oldest, the Next to the Next to the Youngest, the Next to the Youngest, and the Youngest. It could be argued that this father of six sons was not blessed with the greatest imagination, but he at least provided for them, and when the Oldest was 18 and the Youngest was 12 years old, the father sent them out into the world to learn a trade. 'Best you set out together,' he said, and blessed them, and they left the house.

After a while on the trail, the brothers came to a junction where six roads crossed. They decided they would go their separate ways and meet again in three years, in the same place, with their new trades, and would return to their father's house.

What adventures befell them all in those years would take too long to tell, but suffice it to say, they did all turn up at the agreed time and place, and after lots of back-slapping and embraces, they went home to their father. The father asked each one about the trade he had learnt, and was told by the Oldest that he had learned to build ships that could propel themselves, the Next to the Oldest said he had become a helmsman and could steer a ship over both sea and land, the Next to the Next to the Oldest declared he had only learnt to listen but he had developed his listening to such an extent that he could hear what was going on in the next kingdom. The Next to the Next to the Youngest had become a marksman, and whatever weapon he fired, he would never fail to find the target as long as he believed in his aim. The Next to the Youngest had become a skilled climber and no wall or cliff face would daunt him, however high, however sheer, for he had the clever feet of a fly and climbed whatever he wanted without falling.

The father listened to all they had to say, but in his heart, he had held greater hopes for his sons, and so he turned to his favourite youngest son hoping he would make him proudest of all. However, when the Youngest recounted joyously that he had become a master thief, the father could not hide his anger and disappointment. 'You will bring shame on me and this family!' he cried and stormed out.

A short time after, word came to the six brothers that the King's daughter had been kidnapped by a powerful wizard and the reward offered for her rescue was her hand in marriage and half of the kingdom. When the brothers heard this call to adventure, they immediately resolved to try their luck.

The Oldest immediately set about building a ship that went by itself, and when it was built, the Next to the Next to the Oldest listened deeply into the four directions and heard the wizard asleep inside a mountain of glass.

They set their course and sailed there. The Next to the Oldest steered them over the sea and then over the land.

Upon arriving at the mountain, the Next to the Next to the Youngest scrambled up the slippery, slidey ice walls of the mountain. At the top there was a crater, and he looked down into the inside of the mountain, where the wizard slept, with his head in the lap of a tearful Princess. He quickly climbed and slid back down the mountain and then took the Youngest upon his back, scaling the mountain again like a mountain goat. He showed the Youngest the way inside the mountain, and then the master thief set about plying his trade and stole the Princess away without waking the wizard.

They boarded the ship and set sail, but the Next to the Next to the Oldest made sure to continue to listen and narrated the sequence to his brothers. 'The wizard awakes. He yawns and stretches. He sees the Princess is not there. He calls for her. He shouts in rage! He is coming!'

The Princess grew suddenly afraid. 'He will fly fast; he will come after us and kill us all! The only way he can be vanquished is by means of piercing a small black spot in the middle of his chest, and since this is only the size of a freckle, it's impossible to stop him, and our fate is sealed – we are surely doomed!'

Not long after she spoke her fears, the wizard appeared in the sky, like an angry storm cloud broiling in rage. When he spotted the ship, he flew in fury towards them, drawing his wand to send a thunderbolt. But the sharpshooter was ready, took aim, and fired an arrow that precisely pierced the black spot, causing the wizard to shriek in pain and explode into thousands of tiny fragments of fiery shards. These bright, burning residues of the wizard's body we still see in the night sky, as meteorites.

The six brothers then escorted the King's daughter back to her father and there was a great rejoicing in the success of their quest.

After these celebrations, however, the King had a difficult decision to make. Each of the brothers could lay claim to have helped in the rescue of his daughter, and each wanted the prize of her hand in marriage. She too was enamoured with each of them, and her heart could not decide between them.

So, the matter remained unresolved until God intervened with a solution that would prevent any strife growing between them, and one which left a legacy for countless generations. On the next and same night, God sent her old servant Death to visit them all, and then she placed all seven of them in the night sky in the form of a constellation, which we now call the Pleiades. Because of her beauty, God made the Princess the brightest star in the constellation, and because of his age, the master thief was the faintest.

The Hunting of the Great Bear

First Nations, America

There were four hunters who were brothers. No hunters were as good as they at following a trail. They never gave up once they began tracking their quarry.

One day, in the moon when the cold nights return, an urgent message came to the village of the four hunters. A great bear, one so large and powerful that many thought it must be some kind of monster, had appeared. The people of the village whose hunting grounds the monster had invaded were afraid. The children no longer went out to play in the woods. The long houses of the village were guarded each night by men with weapons who stood by the entrances. Each morning, when the people went outside, they found the huge tracks of the bear in the midst of their village. They knew that soon it would become even more bold.

Picking up their spears and calling to their small dog, the four hunters set forth for that village, which was not far away. As they came closer, they noticed how quiet the woods were. There were no signs of rabbits or deer and even the birds were silent. On a great pine tree, they found the scars where the Great Bear had reared up on hind legs and made deep scratches to mark its territory.

The tallest of the brothers tried to touch the highest of the scratch marks with the tip of his spear. 'It is as the people feared,' the first brother said. 'This one we are to hunt is *Nyah-gwaheh*, a monster bear.'

'But what about the magic that the *Nyah-gwaheh* has?' said the second brother.

The first brother shook his head. 'That magic will do it no good if we can find its track.'

'That's true,' said the third brother. 'I have always heard that from the old people. Those creatures can only chase a hunter who has not yet found its trail. When you find the track of the *Nyah-gwaheh* and begin to chase it, then it must run from you.'

'Brothers,' said the fourth hunter, who was the laziest and always hungry, 'did we bring along enough food to eat? It may take a long time to catch this big bear and I'm famished.'

Before long, the four hunters and their small dog reached the village. It was a sad sight to see. There was no fire burning in the centre of the village and the doors of all the long houses were closed. Grim men stood on guard with clubs and spears and there was no game hung from the racks or skins stretched for tanning. The people looked hungry.

The elder of the village came out and the tallest of the four hunters spoke to him. 'Uncle, we have come to help you get rid of the monster.'

Then the laziest of the four brothers spoke, 'Uncle, is there some food we can eat? Can we find a place to rest before we start chasing this big bear? I'm tired.'

The first hunter shook his head and smiled. 'My brother is only joking, Uncle,' he said. 'We are going now to pick up the monster bear's trail.'

'I am not sure you can do that, Nephews,' the elder said. 'For though we find tracks closer and closer to the doors of our lodges each morning, whenever we try to follow those tracks, they disappear.'

The second hunter knelt down and patted the head of their small dog. 'Uncle, that is because they do not have a dog such as ours.' He pointed to the two black circles above the eyes of the small dog. 'This is Four-Eyes, and he can see any tracks, even those that are many days old.'

'May the Creator's protection be with you,' said the elder.

'Do not worry, Uncle,' said the third hunter. 'Once we are on a trail we never stop following until we've finished our hunt.'

'That's why I think we should have something to eat first,' said the fourth hunter, but his brothers did not listen. They nodded to the elder and left the village. Sighing, laziest of the brothers lifted his long spear and trudged after them.

They walked, following their little dog. It kept lifting its head, as if to look around with its four eyes. The trail was not easy to find.

'Brothers,' the fourth and laziest hunter soon began complaining, 'Don't you think we should rest now? We've been walking a long time.'

But his brothers paid no attention to him. Their attention was on the trail. Though they could see no tracks, they were beginning to sense the presence of the *Nyah-gwaheh*. They knew that if they did not soon find its trail, it would make its way behind them and find theirs. Then they would be the hunted ones.

The lazy brother took out his pemmican pouch. At least he could eat while they walked along. He opened the pouch and shook out the dried strips of meat and berries. But instead of the pemmican, pale squirming things fell out into his hands. The magic of the *Nyah-gwaheh* had changed the food into worms.

'Brothers,' he shouted angrily, 'let's hurry up and catch that big bear! Look what it did to my pemmican!'

Meanwhile, like a pale giant shadow, the *Nyah-gwaheh* was moving through the trees close to the hunters. It watched them and its huge teeth shone in its open jaws and its eyes glowed red. It was making its way behind them and would soon be on their trail.

Just then, though, the little dog lifted its head and yelped.

'Four-Eyes has found the trail!' shouted the second brother.

'At last! We have the track of the *Nyah-gwaheh*,' said the third brother.

'Haha, Big Bear!' the lazy one yelled. 'We are after you, now!'

This caused fear in the heart of the great bear for the first time, and it broke into a run. As it left the cover of the pines, the four hunters glimpsed it, a huge pale shape, shining opaquely through the trees. With loud hunting cries, they chased after it.

The great bear's strides were long, and it ran more swiftly than a deer. The four hunters and their little dog were swift also, and they did not fall behind. The trail led through swamps and thickets. It was easy to follow, for the bear pushed everything aside as it ran, even knocking down big trees.

On and on they ran, over hills and through valleys. They came to the slope of a mountain and followed the trail higher and higher, every now and then catching a ghostly glimpse of their quarry over the next rise.

The lazy hunter was getting tired of running, so he pretended to fall and twist his ankle. 'Brothers!' he called out. 'I've sprained my ankle. You must carry me.'

So, his three brothers did as he asked, two of them carrying him by turns while the third hunter carried his spear. They ran more slowly now because of their heavy load, but they were not falling any further behind. The day had turned into night, yet they could still see the flowing white shape of the Great Bear ahead of them.

They were at the top of the mountain now and the ground beneath them was very dark as they ran across it. The bear was tiring, but so were they. It was not so easy to carry their fat and lazy brother. The little dog, Four-Eyes, was close behind the great bear, nipping at its tail as it ran.

'Brothers,' said the lazy one, 'put me down now, I think my leg is better.'

The brothers did as he asked. Fresh and rested, the lazy one grabbed his spear and dashed ahead of the others. Just as the great bear turned to bite at the little dog, he levelled his spear and thrust it into the heart of the *Nyah-Gwaheh*. The monster bear fell dead.

By the time the other brothers caught up, the fattest and laziest hunter had already built a fire and was cutting up the big bear. 'Let's eat, brothers,' he said. 'All this running has made me hungry!'

So, they cooked the meat of the great bear and its fat sizzled as it dripped from their fire. They ate until even the hungriest, laziest one was satisfied, and they all leaned back in contentment. Just then, though, the first hunter looked down at his feet. 'Brothers!' he exclaimed. 'Look below us!'

The four hunters looked down. Far below them were thousands of small sparkling lights in the darkness which, they realized, was now all around them.

'Oh dear! We aren't on a mountain top at all,' said the third brother. 'We are up in the sky.'

And it was so. The Great Bear had indeed been magical. Its trail had taken them high above the earth as it tried to escape the four hunters. However, their determination not to give up the chase had carried them up that strange trail.

Just then their little dog yipped twice.

'Look! The Great Bear!' said the second hunter.

The hunters looked. There, where they had piled the bones of their feast, the Great Bear was coming back to life and rising to its feet. As they watched, it began to run again, the small dog close on its heels.

'Follow me!' shouted the first brother.

Grabbing up their spears, the four hunters again began to chase the Great Bear across the skies.

So it was, the old people say, and so it still is.

Each autumn, the hunters chase the Great Bear across the skies and kill it. Then, as they cut it up for their meal, the blood falls down from the heavens and colours the leaves of the maple trees scarlet. They cook the bear and the fat dripping from their fires turns the grass white.

If you look carefully into the skies as the seasons change, you can read that story. The Great Bear is the square shape some call the bowl of the Big Dipper. The hunters and their small dog (which you can just barely see) are close behind, making the dipper's handle. When autumn comes and that constellation turns upside down, the old people say, 'Ah, the lazy hunter has killed the bear.' But as the moons pass by and the sky moves once more towards spring, the bear slowly rises back on its feet and the chase begins again.

Orion the Hunter

Ancient Greece

Once upon a time, Zeus, the mighty king of the gods, was travelling through the countryside, along with his brothers, Poseidon and Hades. It was getting late, and they were far from any comfort, so they disguised themselves and stopped for the night at a shepherd's house. Not realising the identity of his guests, the old shepherd offered what hospitality he could, made them comfortable, and sacrificed and cooked his last cow for their dinner.

The gods were thankful and impressed by the old man's generosity. They asked him what he desired most in the world. The old shepherd replied that he wished he could have had a son. With a blinding flash of light, Zeus, Poseidon and Mercury revealed themselves and promised to fulfil the old shepherd's wish.

The gods gathered around the hide of the cow that they had just eaten, performed a mystical ceremony, and bundled up the cow skin. They told the old man to wait for three moons before undoing the bundle. A few months later, the old man, with trembling hands, untied the bundle to see a beautiful baby boy inside, smiling up at him. He was overjoyed, and named the boy Orion, meaning 'the light of heaven'.

As Orion grew, he learnt to become a great hunter, and when he was a young man, he came across the seven sisters of the Pleiades. Their beauty was overwhelming to Orion, and with all his ardour he pursued them until Zeus had to intervene, lifting them into the sky out of reach of his unrequited affections.

After that, Orion's reputation as a skilled hunter grew, and attracted the attention of the gods. To please them, Orion provided meat each day for the gods' meals.

One day, Artemis, the moon goddess and goddess of the hunt, asked if she could accompany Orion on his daily hunt. He readily agreed.

The next day, as they were hunting in the woods, they saw a deer. Orion carefully fitted an arrow to his bow and shot. So sure was his aim that the deer died instantly, which pleased Artemis greatly. At dinner that evening, Artemis told the gods of Orion's great ability with the bow. The praise pleased Orion, who vowed to impress Artemis even more the next day.

Arising at dawn, Orion proceeded again to the forest where he shot every animal he came across. He then made a large pile of these animals near the home of Artemis as an offering. Then, knocking on her door, he asked her to come outside and see the great surprise he had for her.

However, upon seeing all the dead animals, Artemis was horrified. She was also the protector of animals and always punished those who killed more than they could eat. In her anger, she stomped her foot on the ground and out of the dust came a great scorpion, which stung Orion on the heel, causing him to die in great pain.

She was then overcome with sorrow and begged Zeus to honour Orion for his great service to the gods by placing his constellation among the most brilliant stars in the sky, where he could remain with his hunting dogs, Canis Major and Minor.

Zeus honoured Orion in this way, depicting him facing the snorting charge of Taurus, the bull. Apollo insisted that the scorpion also be placed in the sky to commemorate the great hunter's downfall. Zeus agreed but placed the scorpion on the opposite side of the sky so, as one rises, the other always sets. He also placed Sagittarius, the Archer, next to the scorpion, with drawn bow aimed at the scorpion's heart, should the scorpion try to advance toward Orion and sting him again.

Four

Creature
Stories

Introduction

To go in the dark with a light is to know the light,
To know the dark, go dark. Go without sight,
And find that the dark too blooms and sings
And is travelled by dark feet and dark wings.

Wendell Berry

Ever since the first 'Once Upon a Time', humanity has animated the world around itself. The living world for our ancestors was more than the living biota of the Earth, it included rocks and landforms, waterways and weather patterns. For our ancestors, all of Creation was alive and sentient, and could be related to as our 'extended family'. Imagine that. You'd never feel lonely!

Needless to say, the universal human tendency to characterise everything, to imbue the animals, rocks and trees with personality and agency, led to a world that was, for them, charged with meaning and texture. The dividing line between people and animals was made porous by this personification. Effectively then, it was a storied world they occupied, with history and geography being espoused in terms of what happened in the story. Mammals, reptiles, amphibians, birds and invertebrates all feature in this grand animation of the human condition, and led to most peoples having a kinship and intimacy with animals that went beyond hunting them for food.

Modernity would be dismissive of such a practice, but to the ancients, they were immersed in a living, breathing, speaking, feeling realm where everything that had matter, mattered. If it had matter, it had spirit. If it had spirit, it deserved respect.

Regardless of whether it's real or imaginary, to my mind anyway, it comes down to choosing which world you wish to belong to. One that is mostly lifeless, or one that is humming and thrumming with life pouring forth out of everything.

The following stories are selected from the vast array of narratives that have creatures as protagonist and/or characters, and which are drawn from a broad range of cultures. It would seem that the impulse to story the world around them was not confined to a small number of traditions. It was universal.

The Fire Quest

Japan

Once upon a time, there was a forest, and in that forest, there was a lake, and on that lake, there was a lotus flower, and this was the home of the Firefly Queen. By day she would rest in the comfort of the lotus petals, and by night she would fly with her dazzling fire, drawing mesmerising patterns of light and hypnotising the other denizens of the dark.

The Firefly Queen had many suitors, such was the seduction of her displays, and innumerable were the constellations of creatures that clustered around her, all desiring of her attention. There were moths, beetles, flies and dragonflies of all shapes and sizes that fluttered and flew over the lake, captivated by her dance. She was haughty and vain, however, and was impervious to their suit. She dismissed them every night, charging them with the task of proving their love to her by bringing her what she most desired. 'If you truly love me, bring me a tongue of flame from a real fire. The one who can bring their passion to me in this form will be deserving of my affections!'

And then there was a great whirring and fluttering of a thousand soft wings as the winged things took to the skies to pursue their fateful love quest. The doomed lovers flew hither and thither in their search for the sacred flame that would bring them their heart's desire. Lured by light, and then bemused and bewitched by the flickering lights of campfire or candlelight, they were driven to destruction in a frantic death-dance denouement. So many perished by flame and firelight, their empty carcasses strewn over the ground to be casually swept away in the morning.

Of those who survived the brightening of the dark, none returned to press their suit with the Firefly Queen. And that may well suit her vanity, for should the flame ever be captured by any other beast, she would not be able to feel her sovereignty over the night.

Spare a thought, though, for the countless beings that stroke the night air with wingbeats, and their tragic allurement to the proliferating artificial lights that humanity has kindled to banish the dark. As you greet the new day each morning, remember that not everything has survived the night, and give thanks.

A Moth Case

Once upon a time, a hunter took his young son with him on the trail. There was no game, and as each day passed it was hard for the young boy to keep up. The rains came, and the land became like a swamp.

And if it was hard before, it was even harder now to find game, or even to travel. Their food supplies dwindled. The boy grew weak, and then sick. The only thing his father could do was to build him a little shelter of bark and tree branches to keep the rain out. The father knew he had to find food for him, so left him tucked up in his kangaroo skin to search for game.

After a short time, or a long time, he returned with a possum he'd speared. He'd hurried back, fearing he'd left him for too long, but was mystified to find his son had gone from the clearing where he'd left him. What's more, the shelter he'd built had also disappeared.

The hunter sensed that there was magic at work. He leaned against a tree, and as he placed his hand against the trunk, the bark was loose, and when he looked closely, he saw a little replica of the shelter he'd built for his son. There were tiny twigs and bark, and when he opened it, he saw inside a little white grub. He knew then that the good spirits had taken pity on the boy and saved him from death in this way. The hunter gave thanks and wept.

To this day, in Queensland, Australia, you will find these little *gunyah* shelters that the case moth builds to protect its larva, just as the father had done for his son.

The Tale of Owl

First Nations, America

In the old days, Owl didn't always stay awake at night. In fact, Owl slept during the hours of darkness. In those days, he was a beautiful day bird, who could sing like the nightingale, and some would say, even better. In fact, Owl was a bird who could do many things better than other birds.

He could fly like an acrobat, he was always successful in the hunt, he was the best student that the old teacher, Wind, had ever had, and Owl knew it. He himself believed there was nothing he could not do better than any other bird.

They admired him, but in his arrogance, he remained aloof from the other birds and would never stop to help them, or even to listen for very long to the wise teachings of the Wind. Despite this, Wind liked Owl very much. She never got angry at him for leaving a class early or flying off to play. Wind knew Owl learned and remembered his lessons faster than any other animal in the woods.

Yet, she did have to warn Owl. She told him to be careful where he flew. She told him not to fly into the Moon's land. 'The Moon is my cousin, and bad things will happen if you stray there,' she warned.

All the creatures of the earth were afraid of Moon. They knew he hated his brother Sun's day-friends. He was jealous of their power to fly wherever they wanted. Birds never flew past the protection of grandfather sky. They even slept at night so as not to see Moon's strange face every night. They knew that just looking into Moon's eyes would probably turn them into stars.

Owl, however, did not believe the stories about Moon. He thought Wind and the other birds and animals were only trying to scare him. One day, he decided to fly higher than he had ever done before. And suddenly, and without knowing how, Owl reached the land of the Moon.

At first Owl was afraid, but nothing happened to him. So, he returned to the Earth realm and boasted of his adventure. He liked going where others had not been, and it gave him a feeling of power and significance. He went again, and again found his way into the land of the Moon. And again, nothing happened to him. Each time he was gone for longer, and each time he went further. Those the Owl left behind were fearful of what Moon might do to punish Owl for his recklessness.

Then, one night, while in the Moon's land, Owl lost his way and did not return. Some say that Moon took him to his lodge and there taught him many things about the dark side. All the birds knew they would never see Owl again and were sorry.

One evening, while all were asleep, they heard a loud piercing cry coming down from the sky. No one would dare leave the safety of their homes to see what was wrong. They were afraid Moon would see them and turn them into a bat or another strange, ugly night creature.

It was Owl, who had been thrown back by the Moon. As he fell to the ground, he screamed, which is when the Moon stole his voice. From that day, Owl could no longer sing like a nightingale, and was bound by enchantment to serve the Moon's bidding. From that time until now, the Owl can be heard only in the night, with only a hoot and a cry to sing of his solitude and sorrow.

How Bat Became

Anishinaabe, Canada/America

Once upon a time, when the earth was very young indeed, the sun rose too close to the Earth and became entangled in the branches of the tall trees of the forest. No matter how he tried, the Sun could not free himself from the thick canopy of twisted, tangled branches, and so on that day, the dawn never came, and the animal people wondered '*why?*'

The next day never came either and the land was under a permanent cloak of night. There was confusion, but some were happy enough, like the Badger and the Owl.

As time passed the animals knew they needed to gather for a council, to see what could be done.

'The Sun is lost, and we must find him,' said Bear.

All animals agreed, and the search began. They looked everywhere, in all the shadowy places, they looked up and down, inside and outside, over and under, but alas, the Sun was nowhere to be found.

When they came together again, the squirrel proposed an idea. 'Perhaps we must look higher not lower. Perhaps I will see from the tops of the tall trees where the Sun is trapped.'

So, Squirrel climbed and scampered her way up and down the tallest trees she could find, until at the top of a very tall tree, deep in the forest, she saw a weak light, entangled in the branches. As she climbed closer, she saw it was indeed the Sun, though his light was now weak and pale.

'Help me, sister Squirrel,' said the Sun, and little squirrel saw what she needed to do. She began to nibble and gnaw the twigs and branches surrounding the Sun. She chomped and chewed, and as she did so, the Sun's light grew stronger and began to scorch and burn Squirrel's fur, until she had to stop.

'I'm nearly free,' said the Sun. 'Can you keep going?'

So, Squirrel began again, nibbling and gnawing, but again stopped in the intensity of heat from the Sun, who was growing stronger, the freer he became.

'Don't stop little Squirrel.'

'I'm growing blind,' she said. 'You are too hot!'

'One more branch, sister!' urged the Sun, and so Squirrel chomped and chewed her way through the last branch, whereupon the Sun rose, magnificent again, into the sky. And daylight shone on the world again.

The animals were delighted that this natural order had been restored, but poor Squirrel was not so happy. She clung to the top of the tree where the Sun had been, unable to move. Her fur was blackened, her tail gone, her eyesight was weak and even her skin had stretched and hung loosely about her body. She was a sorry sight, and the Sun took pity on her.

'Little sister,' he said, 'you have helped me, and now it is my turn to help you. Tell me, what do you need, and I will grant you your wish.'

Squirrel thought long and hard, and she said, 'I can no longer run and climb the trees. I wish then that I could fly instead, like the birds do – I have always wanted to fly.'

'Well, then, let me gather your folds of skin and make them into wings, so that you can fly even better than the birds. Since my light will always now be too bright for your eyes, let me give you ears to see with at night. Let it be so, that you will rise when I am falling, and you will fall away when I rise in the morning. Let go of the branch, little one, and try out your new wings.'

And Squirrel took a deep breath and she let go, and at first, she fell, but she flapped her legs and found that with her skin stretched so thin over her bones, they were now wings, and she flew! And how she could fly!

She was very grateful to the Sun for this great gift of flight, and was happy to fly at night or when the Sun was low. Every time she glimpsed the setting or rising Sun, she would fly with joy in her heart, and she has been flying with joy ever since.

Bat Hides from the Sun

Africa

In the time before time, before the first before, Bat lived with his mother, who one day became ill, and in the following days became even more sick. Bat called Deer to attend to his ailing mother, but Deer took one look at her and said, 'She needs the medicine of the Sun. Only the Sun can help your mother.'

The next day, Bat journeyed to visit the Sun at his house, but it was late morning when he met the sun, already on the road. 'Please help, my mother is sick and needs some medicine,' said Bat.

But the Sun said, 'It is too late, I have already left my house. Come tomorrow.'

So, Bat returned home and slept the night. In the morning, earlier than before, he met the Sun again, already on the road. 'Once I have left my house, I cannot return,' said the Sun. 'That is where I keep the medicine. Come again in the morning.'

Again, Bat returned home, and again he left even earlier the next morning. But again, he was too late. The Sun had already left his house. Each day he tried, each day leaving earlier, and each day he was sent back. His mother grew gravely ill, and by the seventh day, she had died.

Bat was grief-stricken and angry with the Sun. 'If he had made some medicine for her, she would not have died! The Sun is responsible for the death of my mother!'

Many of the beasts came to share in Bat's mourning, and when it was time to bury her, they asked to look upon her face, as they always did before a body went into the grave.

But, when they saw her, they said, 'No, we cannot bury her. She isn't one of us. Look! She has a face like us, but she has wings like a bird. You must call the birds to bury her.' And they left.

Bat called to the birds, and when they looked upon Bat's mother, they saw her teeth and they said, 'Yes, she is like us because she has wings, but look at those teeth! No bird has teeth – she has no beak. We cannot bury her.' And they left Bat alone.

The ants came and entered his mother's body. Bat spoke to himself, 'I blame the Sun. The Sun should have made medicine for my mother. The Sun has killed her. Now the Sun is my enemy, and I will never look upon the Sun's face again, nor will I greet him ever again. I shall hide from the Sun. I will hide in the darkness. I will visit nobody.'

And that is why bats only emerge as the sun is setting, lest they are forced to greet the Sun's smiling face.

Theft of the Sun

Siberia

Once upon a time, it is said by the old ones that darkness came to the land because evil spirits stole the Sun. In the everlasting gloom that followed, they say, all the birds and beasts stumbled about, bumping into things and having to seek their food by touch.

Soon the birds and the beasts decided to call a grand council. A summons was issued, and the animals sent their emissaries to represent them at the council.

The old Raven, who all considered wise, spoke up first, 'My friends, how much longer must we dwell in perpetual darkness? I have asked my ancient knowing and can tell you that not far away, in a great cave, live the evil spirits who have stolen the Sun from us. They keep it in a stone pot. We must go there and steal back the Sun to light up our world again. We must send the strongest to fetch the Sun back. I say, the Bear must go.'

'The Bear! The Bear!' cried all the animals.

At that moment, the ancient, half-deaf Owl noticed all the commotion. Asking the little Cirl Bunting nearby for news, she was told that the Bear was to be sent to fetch the Sun.

'Oh, no, no, no!' cried the Owl. 'That won't do at all. No sooner will he come upon some scrap of food than he'll forget all about his mission. And we'll never get the Sun back.'

With that they all had to agree, 'True enough, the Bear will find some scrap of food and forget about everything else.'

The Raven spoke again, 'Then let's send the Wolf; after the Bear she is the strongest and she is even faster.'

'Yes! The Wolf! Send the Wolf!'

'Fiddlesticks!' snapped the Owl. 'The Wolf is greedy and will stop at the first deer she sees and gobble it up; she'll forget all about the Sun.'

Hearing the Owl's words, the animals had to agree. 'Quite true, quite true,' they said. 'That Wolf is greedy and when she sees a deer, she will stop to kill it, and forget about the Sun. But whom shall we send for the sun?'

Just then a tiny Mouse raised her squeaky voice, 'We should send the Hare, for he is the best runner among all of us; he'll fetch the Sun back for us.'

Once more the birds and beasts cried out, 'Yes! The Hare! The Hare!'

The Owl thought for a bit, then said, 'Yes, he may indeed steal back the Sun. He hops well and skips well and is not selfish. Nobody will be able to catch him.'

So, the Hare was chosen.

Without more ado, the Hare went on his way, guided by the Raven. He hopped and skipped for many days across the land until, at last, he spied a shaft of light far ahead.

As he came closer, he saw that rays of light were coming from under the earth through a narrow crack in some great granite rocks. When he put his eye to the crack, he was able to make out a ball of fire lying in a great stone pot, its fiery rays lighting up a vast underground cavern.

The brave little Hare squeezed through the crack, let himself down on to the floor of the cavern and hopped silently over to the stone pot. He snatched the fireball, hit the ground hard with his hind legs and sprang up through the crack.

At once the evil spirits hollered and screamed and cursed and rushed about trying to squeeze through the crack in pursuit of the Hare.

In the meantime, the little Hare ran as fast as his legs would carry him. However, it was not long before the evil spirits were giving chase, and if the Hare was fast, the evil spirits were faster still. Soon they were right on his heels.

Just as they were about to grab him, he gave the ball of fire a hard kick with his hind legs, breaking it in two: one part small, the other big. With a second kick, he sent the smaller part flying high into the air until it reached the heavens.

And there it became the shimmering silver Moon.

He kicked the big part even higher so that it soared into another region of the sky to become the shining golden Sun.

How bright it became, shining upon the earth.

The evil spirits were blinded by the light and scampered back underground, never to appear on earth again.

And all the birds and the beasts praised the brave little Hare who had rescued the Sun.

And the Moon, in gratitude to the Hare, always keeps an image of the Hare in its house, which you can see when you gaze up at the full moon.

The Hare in the Moon

San Bushman, Kalahari, Namibia

The Moon said to the Hare, 'Go and tell the People that just as I "die" and rise to life again, so shall they die and rise to life again.'

So, the Hare scampered off and presented himself to the People. He told them what he thought the Moon had told him to say: 'Just as the Moon dies, and rises to life again, so you shall die, but you will not rise again.'

The Hare returned to tell the Moon what he'd done, and when the Moon heard this misrepresentation, the Moon took a stick and beat the hare across his face. This is why the Hare has a split lip, and why you always see him running away.

Five

The Coming
of Fire

Introduction

*Among the Dagara, darkness is sacred. It is forbidden
to illuminate it, for light scares the Spirit away ...
The one exception to this rule is the bonfire.*

Malidoma Somé

The relationship between fire and story goes back a long
way. Since the first deliberate kindling of fire, people have
been gathered into the warmth and light from the fireside, which also assured safety from predators. Thus began
an adventure in language and communication. At the end
of the day's activity, the hearth offered rest, comfort and
a freedom from the pressures of a hunting-gathering
lifestyle. With that freedom, the natural emergence was
dialogue and conversation.

As language evolved into more complex speech patterns and extended vocabulary, it's easy to see how the
form of telling each other stories about the day's events
evolved. These stories would have been an essential part
of processing events and wrapping up the day.

Nobody knows this for sure, of course, but it is human
nature to socialise and make relationships through verbal
communication. It would naturally follow, then, that when
these early peoples were blessed with time and leisure
and the impulse to communicate, the sharing around
the campfire would take all sorts of different forms,
from dramatic reportage to funny accounts of what had

transpired that day. Significant past events would have been reprised and told again, and of course, significant dreams would be shared. I wonder if this dream-sharing was the first formal structure of telling narratives.

Either way, the trend developed into the huge variety of forms and genres of stories and storytelling that we see the world over. The stories migrated from their first natural home of fireside telling to appear anywhere and everywhere that people were gathered.

It is fitting, then, given that provenance, that we include some of the following stories, which all feature the element of fire in some way.

How Fire Came Between People and Animals

San Bushman, Kalahari, Namibia

People did not always live on the surface of the Earth. At one time, people and animals lived underneath the Earth with Kaang (Käng), the Great Master and Lord of Creation. In this place, people and animals lived together peacefully. They understood each other. No one ever wanted for anything, and it was always light, even though there wasn't any sun. During this time of bliss, Kaang began to plan the wonders he would put in the world above.

First, Kaang created a wondrous tree, with branches stretching over the entire country. At the base of the tree, he dug a hole that reached all the way down into the world where the people and animals lived. After he had finished furnishing the world as he pleased, he led the first man up the hole. He sat down on the edge of the hole and then the first woman came up out of it. Soon, all the people were gathered at the foot of the tree, awed by the world they had just entered.

Next, Kaang began helping the animals climb out of the hole. In their eagerness, some of the animals found a way to climb up through the tree's roots and come out of the branches. They continued racing out of the world beneath until all the animals were out.

Kaang gathered all the people and animals about him. He instructed them to live together peacefully. Then, he turned to the men and women and warned them not to build any fires or a great evil would befall them. They gave their word and Kaang left to where he could watch his world from a secret place.

As evening approached, the sun began to sink beneath the horizon. The people and animals stood watching this phenomenon, but when the sun disappeared fear entered the hearts of the people. They could no longer see each other as they lacked the eyes of the animals that could see in the dark. They lacked the warm fur of the animals and soon grew cold.

In desperation, one man suggested that they build a fire to keep warm. Forgetting Kaang's warning, they disobeyed him. They soon grew warm and were once again able to see each other.

However, the fire frightened the animals. They fled to the caves and mountains and ever since the people broke Kaang's command, people have not been able to communicate with animals.

Now, fear has replaced the seat of friendship once held between the two groups.

A Fire Tail

In the time before time, so long ago that the time could only be counted by suns or moons, a band of Cowichan Indians was drying deer meat in the morning sun. It had been a very cold night, and they spoke of how good it would be to have their own 'small sun' to warm them when the big sun left them to the night's cold embrace. They had nothing else, for this was so long ago that people did not know how to make fire. Of course, they knew they were only dreaming out loud because to have that, it would take power and magic to obtain, and not one of their shamans had that much power.

As they wished and talked, they suddenly noticed a little bird who was calling close by. They did not recognise its call, and this was unusual. So, they stopped talking and gave it their attention, and more so when it flew closer to them. They saw that it was a beautiful brown bird with a bright red tail, which seemed to shimmer and shine even when the bird sat still. They were mesmerized by this flickering red and orange light on its tail as this curious creature hopped from branch to branch, until the bird looked down on them from a branch right above their heads.

The oldest man spoke the languages of birds, and he greeted the bird in the old way, praising its song and its plumage. 'What do you want, little bird?' he asked.

'Nothing do I wish for myself, but I can bring you what you would dearly wish,' it replied.

'How so?' said the old man.

'Do you see my tail?' said the bird. 'It is hot and bright like the flaming feathers of the sun. I can make you a gift of this, which will comfort you when the north winds of winter blow, that will cook your meat and bring light and cheer when the sun sinks below the ground.'

'That would be a great gift!' said the old man. 'My people surely need this to ease their suffering in the long cold nights of winter.'

'Well, if you want it, you must earn it,' said the little bird. 'Tell your hunters to meet me here at dawn and ask each one to bring a little dry branch with pitch pine on it.'

The bird then disappeared, and the old man said to his companions, 'We should follow up that invitation, it may bring us good fortune.'

When the sun shone again, the hunters waited in the same spot, as invited by that strange little bird. Each carried a branch with pitch pine on it, as they had been told. With no warning, suddenly the brown bird was perched on a branch above them.

It asked in a language that, this time, all could understand, 'Are you ready?'

They answered, 'Yes!'

'Then you must follow me, if you can, and the one who first catches up with me will be given the gift of fire from my tail, but only if the one who does so is respectful, is patient, and tries hard without losing faith or courage. Come! Let's go!'

The bird flew off over the rough ground and thick forest. The chase was long, and it was difficult for the hunters to keep pace with it as it darted between the trees. For many, the going was too tough, and they fell away. Over fast-flowing streams and then marsh and swamp, the little bird continued to fly, perching occasionally on the rocks and the branches to keep the hunters interested.

As the chase went on, more hunters dropped out. By now, there were only a few left in the chase. At last, one young warrior got close enough to call to the bird. He was hot, and tired and somewhat frustrated and even angry. 'Give me your fire, you miserable little bird. I have followed you far and I deserve the prize for I am the strongest!'

'I shall not,' said the bird, flying higher. 'You think only of yourself. You shall not have the prize.'

A second young man caught up with the bird. 'Give your fire to me,' he called. 'I have followed with faith and courage, and I am the best warrior and I deserve the reward. It will make me stronger to have it.'

'A good man does not simply take that which belongs to another, for his own ends,' the bird answered, flying faster and faster.

Soon, when it was no longer being followed, the little bird flew to the ground and perched on a branch above a woman who was sitting against the trunk of the tree below, nursing an old man who looked very frail and sick. The bird cocked its head onto one side and watched her for a while tending to the sick man. Then, it opened its beak and called for her attention.

'You, who take good care of others, I have treasure to share with you. Bring a branch with pitch pine on it,' said the bird. 'I have fire on my tail, and you shall have it to keep your sick friend warm and to cook your food, and to bring you comfort at night.'

The woman was afraid, at first, of a bird that could speak. She said, 'I don't deserve such a magical gift. I do this because it is the right thing to do. We people take care of those who are sick.'

'You are a good woman, thinking of others,' said the bird. 'Now, do the thing that will bring your people much happiness. Fetch a branch and take of my fire and bring this precious gift to your people.'

The woman then brought a branch and kindled it from the little fire that flickered on the bird's tail. She walked with it back to her people and she shared it with them. And so, the first flames were brought to the first people.

That was all long ago, and since that time, those first people who lived in the wild world have had fire to keep them warm and cook their food. And they've been singing the praises of the birds ever since!

Grandmother Spider Fetches Fire

Choctaw, America

The Choctaw people remember that when the world was young all people were related, and as well as two-legged ones, there were also four-legged ones, and winged ones and those with fur or scales. They remember that all of these 'first people' came up from the ground, and they were encased in cocoons, with their eyes closed, and their limbs and wings were tightly folded around their bodies. They were all there in the ground until the Great Spirit brought them up and released them from their cocoons and opened their eyes. The world then, however, was cold, and dark.

The Animal People and the Human People crawled around, feeling their way, eating anything that did not eat them first. Life was hard, and not to anyone's satisfaction. So, they held their first council, and discussed how things might be changed. One of the voices said, 'I have been over to the East, and farther than far over there, the people have a great fire. It is bright, and warm.' This notion was new to many and caused a great wonderment among them.

Another voice said, 'But those people in the East guard it, and won't give it away.'

'Then we will have to steal it!' said another voice, out of the darkness, and there was a chorus of approval.

The question was then asked, 'Who can do this? Which of us has what it takes to go there and bring back this essential treasure?'

Grandmother Spider was the first to speak into the long pause that followed. 'I will go,' she said. 'I will do this for all the People.' But then Opossum spoke up. 'I am the best hunter, and I have the best and bushiest tail for this. I will steal some fire and hide it in my tail. So, it should be me who goes.'

So, it was agreed, and Opossum travelled through the endless dark until he came to the East and saw with awe the great burning bonfire and he was amazed. He also saw the jealous People guarding their fire. Opossum, using shadow and silence, managed to slip between them, and take a piece of burning wood. He stuck it on the end of his tail, but his tail caught fire, and the People of the East saw him and chased him and took back the burning wood and drove Opossum away.

Poor Opossum returned to the council and showed them his tail, which even today, still has no fur on it. The council had to choose someone else, and Grandmother Spider again said, 'Let me go! I will try', but again her small voice was relegated behind a more powerful voice instead.

Eagle put himself forward this time, and persuaded the council he had the necessary strength and endurance to go there, 'And I will carry the fire back in my long feathers.'

So, Eagle flew East on his broad wings and then swooped down to scoop up some embers. He placed them in his long feathers that he wore on his head, but soon these feathers caught alight, and the People of the East chased him away. He returned, chastened, to the council with his head burnt red and bald – his feathers never grew back, which is why you still see the baldness of the Eagle today.

Now the Animal People began to understand there was more to this fire element than they had bargained for. Since ancient times, people have relied on the cleverness of Crow to help them out of challenging situations, and so again they ignored the Grandmother Spider volunteering to go and sent instead the sweet-voiced crow.

In those days, not only did Crow have white feathers, but he also had lovely songs. But, when Crow arrived, he spent too long hovering over the fire so that his feathers were burnt black and his voice became all croaky in the smoke. A blackened Crow returned to the council and could only say, 'Caw!' And he's been singing 'Caw!', and only 'Caw!', ever since.

Finally, the council agreed to send Grandmother Spider. She had already figured out her strategy, and scuttled away to the stream where she knew she would find clay to make a small pot, with a tight-fitting lid. Balancing the pot on her back, she then travelled East, and it took her longer than those who had gone before.

When she finally arrived and saw the fire, she wove herself a web, and then waited in it while she figured out how she would collect the fire. At length, she saw how to sneak past the guards, and when she approached the edge of the fire, she scraped some embers into her pot, which she duly carried all the way back.

When the People first saw her returning, they said, 'She has failed, there is no fire,' but when Grandmother Spider got closer, they saw wisps of smoke coming out of a little hole she'd left in the pot lid. They all gathered around the clay pot, as Grandmother Spider lifted the lid to reveal the embers, and when the embers met the air, they kindled into flame, and the animal people marvelled to see its flames burning the darkness from the sky, and they felt its warmth and they took pleasure in it.

But then they had to decide which of them would take it out of the pot. Bear immediately reached forward. 'I'll take it,' he said, but then burnt his paw when he tried. 'Oww! This is not for the Animal People,' he said, and they agreed as they all remembered what had also happened to Opossum.

The Bird People also declined, as Eagle and Crow were still nursing their wounds. The same went for the Reptile, Amphibian and Insect People, who all recognised the danger from the fire.

In the end, the timid voice of the Human People was heard to say, 'Maybe we should take it?' It was agreed among the Animals and Grandmother Spider to show the Two-Legged People how it could be kindled with more sticks, and how to keep it safely contained. After that, she showed them how to make clay pots, and after that, she taught them how to weave.

That is why the Choctaw people remember to honour Grandmother Spider for all the gifts she brought to them, and you can see her image represented in the things they make and weave.

Bokka Fetches Fire

Romany Gypsy

The first people were nomads. They wandered the wild world and were blessed with an abundant harvest of food. The Romany Gypsies continue to roam the highways and byways, through all the weather and the everlasting cycle of seasons.

In the long winters of the north, they still tell the story of how it was they sustained themselves during the cold, dark nights and days of winter. It was all to do with Bokka, who fetched fire from the gods. This is how he did it.

In those days, the gods warmed themselves at night with campfires they lit from the setting sun, at the edge of the world. They were indifferent to the suffering of the people, who were miserable in the biting cold of winter because there was nothing to keep them warm. They would huddle together at night, and gaze up at the fierce, distant sparkling stars and dream of the return of the sun. 'If only the gods would give us just a small piece of the sun,' they would say. But despite their prayers and protestations, they knew there was no persuading the mean and inconsiderate gods.

One day, a young man called Bokka, the son of a wagon wheelmaker, overheard his elders bemoaning the onset of winter and resolved to help. 'I will make representation to the gods. I will go and ask them myself. Nobody else seems to even try anymore.' The elders told him he would be wasting his time; his older brothers merely mocked his impulse.

Bokka, though, had always been a determined boy, and the more he thought about it, the more he believed in the quest. At length, he packed a few provisions, hugged his mother and set off on the trail.

Bokka travelled for many days, travelling the beaten paths and unbeaten paths, over hills and hollows, mountains and moorland, fields and forests. One day, while walking across some fields, he heard a voice call out from a barn that he was passing, It was a small voice, and he heard it calling out to him, 'Good sir, please help me!'

Bokka stopped and peered into the building. The barn was filled with grain sacks and in front of these were several traps and caught in one of these traps was a black rat. 'Did you call out to me?' asked Bokka.

The rat cried, 'Yes! Please help me out of the farmer's trap. You are a Romany so you will know the sweet taste of freedom.'

'I do indeed,' replied Bokka. 'But I wouldn't have got caught in the first place!' He then glanced at the plentiful supply of grain sacks. 'Were you taking the farmer's grain?'

The rat replied, 'Yes, there's so much here, the farmer should not begrudge me a small amount.'

Bokka agreed with this, knelt down and released the black rat from the trap. Rather than running off, the rat said, 'Thank you for this kindness. Now, tell me where you are going, and perhaps I can do you a good turn.'

Bokka told the rat of his quest to find the gods to request a piece of the sun, so that his people could keep warm.

'Well then,' said the rat. 'My name is Yag and because I am in your debt, allow me to ride on your shoulder so that I may help you when you are in need.'

Bokka liked the idea of company, and gently lifted the rat, placed him on his shoulder and set off again.

After a while, they entered a huge forest, and after some days travelling through the tangle of trees, they came to a clearing where Bokka and Yag saw a ring of big, brightly coloured, carved wooden wagons with potent and mysterious designs painted on their sides. Bokka had never seen such large and beautiful wagons before, and he was mesmerised by their appearance in the middle of an ancient forest. He hid at the edge of the clearing to observe for a while.

He saw that, in the middle of the circle, the gods themselves were sitting, eating and drinking, laughing and singing, toasting and boasting. But what caught Bokka's attention even more than this was the bright, flickering, dancing, yellow light in the middle of the gods. It was burning hot, warming the gods, and Bokka knew that this was what he was seeking, a piece of the sun.

Above it, suspended on a tripod, there was a pot of bubbling, boiling water, and next to this were long skewers on which they were roasting rabbits, squirrels and hedgehogs. The aroma was delicious, and Bokka's mouth watered, and his stomach rumbled. He was so hungry, and before he could stop himself, he'd walked out of the shadows of the trees and into the circle, much to the surprise of the gods.

'Greetings, oh mighty ones,' Bokka said, bowing down before them. 'I am so very humbled to stand before your might and majesty.'

The gods seemed pleased with this courtesy, and so he continued. 'I have come a long way in search of a piece of the sun to bring back for my people. They suffer greatly in the cold and the dark nights of winter and will be grateful to you forever to receive this precious gift.'

One of the gods, the oldest woman, who had an ancient face wrinkled like the skin of an old apple, looked at Bokka with her piercing bright green eyes and said, 'You may tarry for a while and eat and drink with us. But know this, you are forbidden to take anything away with you.'

Bokka was very hungry and so he gratefully accepted the invitation to eat, and soon was filling his belly, while Yag scurried and scampered around to rummage for whatever he could find on the ground to eat. The gods looked curiously upon this and on the young Roma.

At length, Bokka stood to take his leave, and asked again if he could bring back a piece of the sun for his people, but again the gods declined his request and turned back to their feasting. Bokka was downhearted as he walked away and was not looking forward to the mockery from his brothers when he returned empty-handed. He felt a failure.

He noticed then that he was without his little companion, and he turned to call his friend. He saw the black rat bustling around, and then running towards him with a long stalk of fennel that he'd picked up from the ashes of the fire. This seemed to make the gods laugh, 'Your little friend must be hungry,' they said. 'Let him keep it.'

As Yag approached, Bokka noticed a small trail of smoke curling up from the end of the stalk. The soft pith core was still smouldering with the fire from the sun.

'Let us hurry,' said Yag. 'If we are quick, we can carry this back to light the first fire for your people.'

The two friends raced off immediately, and in half the time it took Bokka to reach the circle of gods, he was entering his own circle of wagons, surrounded by his people, who were eager to hear his news.

Carefully, Bokka blew upon the smouldering fennel until there was a nice glowing ember. This was used to light some straw and then kindle some small sticks. Shortly afterwards, a great pile of sun's fire was blazing away in the Gypsy camp.

The people sat around late into the night, mesmerised by the tongues of flame burning the darkness from the sky. Bokka told them his story, and the clever rat's role in bringing the fire home.

This was the first story told around the first fire and the Romany people have been telling stories around camp-fires ever since. In gratitude to the rat, the Romany word for fire is *yag*.

Rainbow Crow

Lenni-Lenape, Canada/America

Long ago, when the world was being made, our ancestors were animals and all the animals could speak to one
another. There came a time when soft, glittering, ice-cold
flakes fell from the sky. At first, there was wonder at such a
marvel. Then there was joy as the animals ran about catching the flakes to melt them in their mouths. But then there
was misery, as the flakes piled up higher and higher, the
ground became frozen and the air was cold.

It became a time of suffering for the animals, as many
of the smaller creatures were disappearing under the thick
blanket of cold snow, for that was what it was. All that
could be seen of the Rabbit, for example, was the tips of
his ears.

So, the animals met in a council to decide what to do.
They decided a message had to be sent to the Creator,
Kishelamàkänk, who dwelt in the far distant twelfth
realm, the other side of the sky.

'Who should we send on such a journey?' wondered the
animals and looked among themselves for a messenger.

Opossum suggested that Owl should go, as she was the
wisest, but the Owl was reluctant to go in the brightness
of the day.

Beaver proposed then that Racoon was clever, but then
realised without wings it might be too far to travel.

Skunk was keen for Coyote to go, 'because she is so full of tricks!' But the animals decided Coyote was too easily distracted.

And so the process continued, and still snow piled upon snow, and some of the smaller animals, like Mouse, climbed on the backs and heads of the taller animals so they wouldn't disappear.

Just as they were giving voice to their despair in squeaks, howls, grunts and barks, there was a flash of bright colours and Crow flew into the gathering. In those days, Crow had beautiful, coloured feathers, like a rainbow, and he sang the sweetest of all songs.

When Rainbow Crow heard of the quest, he volunteered to go, much to the relief and joy of the council, who praised his courage and kindness. Rainbow Crow flew up into the swirling snow and rode the air till he was above the clouds, and flew further, until he was beyond the moon, and after three days, he arrived in the twelfth realm.

Kishelamàkänk was nowhere to be seen, and so Rainbow Crow opened his beak and began to sing a song of such sweetness that Kishelamàkänk soon appeared and sat enraptured before the bird. When Rainbow Crow stopped singing, the Creator begged him not to stop. Rainbow Crow said, 'I will gladly sing for you again, but perhaps in exchange, you will help us?'

'If it is within my power, I will,' said Kishelamàkänk. 'Tell me, what is it you need?'

'You have to make the snow go away,' said Rainbow Crow.

'Ah, but the snow has a spirit of its own,' said Kishelamàkänk. 'I cannot make it disappear. You will have to wait for the Wind Spirit to move it along. This will happen in time, don't worry.'

'Well, then,' replied Rainbow Crow, 'can you at least stop the cold?'

'That, too, is impossible for me to do,' said Kishelamàkänk. 'However, I can give you a gift to take away that will make it more bearable. Sing me one more song, and then I will give it to you.'

So, Rainbow Crow obliged and then the Creator produced a stick and stuck it into the Sun. When the stick was flaming, he said, 'Take this back to your people. It will keep them warm and melt the snow. I will give you this gift only once so take care of it. Hurry before the fire goes out!'

Rainbow Crow flew off and made the journey back to his people. On the way back, the smoke from the burning stick blackened all his feathers, and when he was close to home, the stick had burnt down and was hot to carry in his beak. But carry it he did, brave bird, and the smoke and hot ashes fell into his throat until all he could produce by way of a voice was, 'Caw! Caw!'

This was a testament to his courage, and when he flew down to set the very first fire alight, the animals were so grateful to him and so sorry about what it had cost him.

The snow was melted, and it felt warm by the fire. The animals praised Rainbow Crow for bringing this amazing gift, but Rainbow Crow was miserable and flew off to perch by himself in the bare branches of a distant tree. Here, he wept for the loss of his rainbow cloak of feathers and the sweetness of his song. No longer could he be called Rainbow Crow, he was now just Crow, and that is what he has been called ever since. He wept for a long time.

Kishelamàkänk heard this sorrow and manifested before him. When he understood what had happened, he said, 'Soon two-legged people will come and take fire from the animals and become master of everything. But you will always be free. I will give this gift of freedom, and people won't pursue you, because your flesh now tastes like smoke, and they will never cage you because your voice is harsh upon his ear. He won't want your feathers either, because they are now black. But you will see, if you look closely, they still have colours hidden there.'

Rainbow Crow looked down at his feathers and saw tiny rainbows glistening, and this cheered him up. Kishelamàkänk returned to the realm beyond the sky, and Crow returned to his people, content that he was a bird coloured like the night, and yet, for those with eyes to see, his feathers shimmered with tiny rainbows.

The Gift from Prometheus

In those ancient times there were two brothers, who were not men, but who were not gods either. They were the sons of the Titans, who'd fought with the gods and who were in exile, banished to the Lower World. For some reason, these two brothers had been spared this punishment and were free to wander at will.

The eldest was called Prometheus, meaning 'forethought'. This was because he was always thinking of the future and making things ready for what might happen tomorrow, or next week, or next year, or even a hundred years to come.

The younger brother was called Epimetheus, meaning 'afterthought'. He was so named because he was always busy thinking of the past and what had happened yesterday, or last year, or a hundred years ago. He had no thought for the future, as that was his brother's preoccupation.

The eldest did not care for the mountain top, the domain of the gods, and spurned their idle ways of drinking nectar and eating ambrosia. Instead, he preferred to wander the Earth among the lives of people.

There he saw how miserable they were, especially in the wintertime. They were cold and hungry and eking out their lives hunting and gathering, but without joy.

He felt sadness and his impulse was to help them take care of their future. He went straight to the mountain top to find Zeus, the supreme god, and asked for the gift of fire to give to the people.

Zeus was unmoved. 'If we give this to them, it will make them stronger and who knows where that will lead? Let them live like the beasts. Not a single spark will I give!'

Thus was Prometheus turned away, and one day while he was walking along and wondering how he could bring fire to the people in spite of Zeus, he absent-mindedly plucked a fennel stalk and when he had broken it off, he saw that its hollow centre was filled with a dry, soft pith which he imagined would burn slowly. He took the long stalk to the top of Mount Olympus, reached it out towards the sun and, sure enough, it caught fire and slowly smouldered. He hastened down the mountain with the precious ember and called the people from their caves. He showed them how to build a fire from the burning coal and soon there was a bright blaze.

The people gathered around and were entranced by the dancing flames. As the sun set, they felt its warmth and watched flames brighten the dark. Around the fire, they felt safe from the wild beasts and soon they learned to cook their food.

They gave thanks to Prometheus, who had presented them with a gift that would take care of their future.

Zeus, however, had been outsmarted and was outraged. He condemned Prometheus to eternal torment for this and various other transgressions. To this day, Prometheus is chained to a rock and suffers his liver being eaten every day by a monstrous eagle.

But the people did indeed grow stronger with the advent of fire. Some say it led to them chasing the gods from their mountain home, which is why you don't see them up there anymore.

Six

Ghost
Stories

Introduction

In a dark time, the eye begins to see.

Theodore Roethke

Fear of the dark has its provenance in our biology. Our dominant sense is our sight, and therefore we feel unsettled if deprived of this orientation. Combined with a history of not being the apex predator, we have good reason for our mistrust of the dark. There were, and in some regions of the world still are, creatures that might leap out of the dark to eat you. That was enough information to maintain a keen interest in the night, and of course, a bright campfire was our sanctuary from those threats.

It is curious, then, how we entertain ourselves with stories about dark and sinister events, hauntings and happenings, the like of which are presented here in this brief anthology from the genre of ghost stories. It's only the briefest of glimpses into a vast repository of tales, real or imagined, whose sole intention is to frighten you. Our contemporary multimillion-pound industry of horror movies proves the point again – we just love being scared. We'll even pay for it!

As a storyteller, the stories I'm asked for most often by kids are ghost stories. To underline our fascination with being frightened, when I've finished one story, the question that invariably follows is, 'Have you got a scarier one?'

Here's a few, then, from a treasure trove of troubling tales. I hope you are not too troubled by them!

Old Crooker

Once upon a springtime, there was a weary traveller making his way on an unfamiliar road to Cromford, late in the evening, when he came across an old woman carrying a posy of St John's wort. 'Where are you bound, good sir?' she asked. 'The night approaches and this is no road to travel in the dark.'

'Why is that?' asked the traveller.

'Because of the Crooker,' she replied. 'Wait a minute, I recognise you. I saw you once rescue a duck caught in a fowler's net. For that act of kindness, I'll give you this bouquet, and then you can show it to Crooker if he appears. Pray that he doesn't, but at least now you have something to offer him.'

She thrust it into his hands and disappeared into the gathering gloom of the dusk.

The traveller went on his way, somewhat unsettled by the idea of meeting Crooker, whoever he was.

Not long after that, he came across another old woman at the side of the road, bearing a posy of yellow primroses. She too asked his destination and then warned him of the danger in being on the Cromford road at night. And then she said, 'I recognise you, sir. I saw you free a rabbit from a snare. For your compassion, I will help you. If you meet a dark stranger tonight, show him these flowers, and you'll have safe passage.'

'What stranger?' asked the traveller, 'You mean Crooker?' But it was too late, for she'd bustled away into the deepening dark.

Now the traveller was distinctly unsettled with the prospect of meeting this unsavoury-sounding fellow, but travel on he must.

A short way down the road, another shadowy figure appeared, and he was surprised to see a third old woman waiting on the verge. She carried a posy of white ramsons and immediately urged him caution. ''Tis a moonless night, and old Crooker loves the dark. Take these and when he comes, you must show them to distract him.'

'Thank you,' said the traveller. 'But please tell me, who is this Crooker?'

The old woman did not answer this, instead she said, 'I do believe I know you. I saw you once free a vixen and her cub from a trap, and for that I'll give you another bit of advice. Keep as far away from Darrent River as you can, for she is in spate after the rain, and be very sure to get to Cromford Bridge before moonrise.' And with that, she was off scurrying into the night.

The traveller continued his journey, but now with much trepidation. As he approached Cromford Bridge, the moon made an appearance, rising above the hills, and the traveller quickened his step. Ahead he saw the sinister silhouette of a large, overhanging tree casting its shadow over the road, shadows that shivered in the night breeze, and which unnerved the traveller.

He pressed on, running the gauntlet of shadows, and as he did so, more shadows appeared and, what's more, they seemed to follow him. When he heard the River Darrent moaning, 'Hungry! Hungry!', he hastened his step, at which point a shadow seemed to step out in front of him. Terrified, he flung the first posy at the shadow, and hurried past.

Another shadow clutched at him, screeching, 'Hungry! Hungry!' and he flung the second posy and ran on.

As he approached the bridge, with the river thrashing its turbulence underneath, moaning and groaning, another pair of shadowy arms reached out, crying, 'Hungry! Hungry!' The traveller, weary no longer, flung the final bunch of flowers at the wickedness and leaped for the safety of the bridge. There, he fell to his knees at the shrine built there and clasped his hands together in prayer, giving thanks for making it through, and looking back at the sinister dance of shadows behind him.

He went on his way, and the further he got away from those trees and shadows, the more his fear subsided, and the more he questioned his grasp on reality. 'Was that a lucid nightmare?' he mused.

In the meantime, under the moonlight in the churchyard, three old women were talking in low voices. 'Crooker is abroad this night, and the river is hungry,' said one.

'We should fetch the priest as soon as the sun is up,' said another.

'There'll be yet another to bury in the cold ground,' said the third.

But there wasn't. Not that night, anyway.

The Death Coach

It's a funny old place, Devon. I don't know what it is about these ancient hills that give rise to so many strange and sinister goings on. Maybe it's the funny folk that live there? Whichever way you look at it, there is no denying the multitude of accounts of hauntings and happenings all over the shire. You've only got to visit the libraries of Exeter or Plymouth to read all the articles and testimonies of the sightings and visitations and general other-worldliness to find out for yourself ...

And of all accounts, the most frequent and perhaps the most sinister of all of them is that of the Death Coach, sighted most often on Dartmoor between Okehampton and Tavistock. It is compelling to note that they report on some common features: it's black all over; it's drawn by four or six black horses; it's driven by a headless coachman; there's, more often than not, a big black dog in the vicinity; and inside the coach sits a shadowy female figure.

Now, this figure is reportedly a certain Lady Howarth, who lived in the sixteenth century, surviving four husbands and two children, all of whom died in 'mysterious circumstances'. Popular opinion credited her with their murders, and it is said that her penance is to drive nightly over the moors to convey a blade of grass from Okehampton Park to Fitsford, and to continue to do so until all the grass has been plucked – at which point, the world will be at an end.

So, be careful if you are abroad at night on Dartmoor, just in case you hear the rumble of wheels and see the dark shape of the coach approaching. If you do, best pray hard that it passes you by, for it is said that the coach only stops to pick up the spirits of those about to die …

The Ballad of Lady Howard

My Lady hath a sable coach
And horses two and four.
My Lady hath a black bloodhound
That runneth on before.
My Lady's coach hath nodding plumes
The driver hath no head.
My Lady's face is ashen white
As one that is long dead.
'Now pray step in,' my Lady said,
'Pray step in and ride.'
'I thank thee, I'd rather walk
Than gather to your side.'
The wheels go round, without a sound
Or turn or tramp of wheels.
As cloud at night in pale moonlight
Along the carriage steals.
I'd rather walk a hundred miles
And run by night and day
Than have that carriage halt for me
And hear my Lady say,
'Now pray step in, and make no din
Step in with me and ride.
'There's room, I trow, by me for you
And all the world besides.'

A Stick of Blackthorn

Ireland

Death seems to be the end of all things. 'One thing and one thing only is certain in life,' the old folk say, 'and that is that it all ends – for death comes to visit everyone, rich or poor.' But there are those who say it is but a beginning, and this, of course, offers a crumb of comfort to those left behind with nothing but grief and memories to console them.

The story starts in the strangest of places – neither at the beginning nor at the end but betwixt the two – at a funeral in Ireland, where there is a tradition of holding a wake for all who care to attend. Here, the line between commiseration and celebration is thin, as the Guinness flows and the girls flirt and the old men are flatulent, and everyone indulges in grief, gossip and gluttony.

The setting is first the churchyard where old Seamus is being buried, and then the solemn procession proceeds to his widow's cottage, where everyone remembers his life and loves, and forgets his mistakes and misdemeanours.

There is one old man sitting in the corner and there are three young girls with nothing better to do than tease him for his affections, in the way that girls of a certain age do – well, in Ireland anyway. 'Oh, to be sure,' said one, 'I'd marry you tomorrow, for I bet you have a wee bit tucked away.'

'Don't you find me prettier than she?' said another. 'I'd marry you for love not money!'

'Well,' he says, 'I'd marry you all if I could, but above all else I'd marry the girl who's got spirit!'

'Oh sir,' one replied, 'I have a generous helping o' that!'

'No sir,' said another, 'I think you'll find that I'm blessed with a cartload more than she.'

'Well, then,' said the old fellow, 'I'll marry the girl who's willing to fetch me my old blackthorn stick I left stuck in the ground in the churchyard.'

By this time it was twilight already, and it was a fair way up there, and the three set off, giddy and giggling, and making their way along the green lane toward the church.

But bravado was soon on the wane as the gloom and mist wrapped around them, and their conversation turned towards what they themselves had left behind, and so two of them decided to turn back. But the one called Mary teased them about their lack of spirit and how she would win the old man's fortune and was resolved to complete the errand. 'Mind you,' she said, 'if I'm not back by midnight, come and get me!' and she watched her companions scurry off, sniggering, into the dusk.

As Mary arrived at the church, a mist was shrouding the graveyard, and there was an eerie stillness. Her confidence was beginning to ebb away as she entered the hallowed ground, but she pressed on.

As she walked, she peered among the many gravestones jutting up from the turf, until she saw the stick planted into the soil above a recently turfed grave. She grasped it firmly and pulled it, but no sooner had she pulled it than she felt it being tugged back down. She let go with a shriek, and then heard a muffled voice from beneath her feet.

'Fetch me out of the ground!' it said.

Common courtesy merits a reply, so she said, 'I will not!'

The voice then commanded her, 'You must, and you shall!'

So, she found herself on her knees obeying, for the voice of the dead can be compelling. She pulled back the turf and saw an aged coffin.

'Lift the lid!' said the voice from inside the coffin.

'I will not!' she replied again.

'You must and you shall!'

So, she obeyed and lifted the lid and inside saw a twisted, thin, blackened corpse of an old man, skin stretched taught over his spindly frame and with hollow eye sockets, which looked at her and said, 'Fetch me up onto your back!'

'I will not!' she said, appalled.

'You must and you shall!' he insisted. Thus, she was compelled, and she shuddered as she hoisted the foul, rank, smelly corpse onto her back.

'Now let's pay a visit – carry me to the nearest cottage,' said the corpse.

The girl staggered along, piggy-backing the corpse on her back as it muttered directions into her ear, until they arrived at an old one-up-one-down cottage, which belonged to the Flattery brothers.

All was quiet, except for the faint sound of snoring coming from upstairs where the brothers were asleep in bed.

'Enter!' said the corpse, and she lifted the latch and the old door swung open, creaking on its hinges and they entered the kitchen. The corpse said, 'Now, I'm hungry!

Bake me some oatmeal bread. But no lights!'

So, Mary rummaged around in the darkness for the oatmeal, but she could not find any milk.

'Use water instead,' said the old corpse.

But the brothers had not fetched water, so she said, 'There is none, good sir!'

'Well, then,' said the old man, 'there's a price for laziness – for we must have liquid for the bread.' Whereupon he slithered off her back, picked up the kitchen knife and crawled up the wooden stairs.

If there was a moment to flee, this was it, but Mary felt strangely fixated on the outcome of the evening, and after what sounded like a splutter and a scuffle, he came downstairs and in his bony hands he carried a bedpan, and that bedpan was full of warm blood.

'There, now, we have our liquid! Get on with it!'

Mary was horrified, but did as she was told, and mixed the blood with the oatmeal and she lit the stove, and as she was working, the moonlight streaming in the tiny window, the corpse gazed at her and after a while, it said, 'A pity those wretched brothers didn't know there was gold buried under the blackthorn tree at the top of their field.'

Mary heard, but did not respond, focusing on her morbid task, and sooner than she would have liked, she had baked the bread and they sat at table.

'Eat!' said the corpse.

'I will not!' said Mary.

'You must and you shall!' he commanded, and so she lifted the oatcake to her mouth, but pretended to eat instead, and let lumps of the bread fall into her lap. These she secreted away in her pocket while the corpse also fed on the blood and oats. 'This will put life back into the dead,' he said and immediately a change came over him. His cheeks suffused with blood, and he was filled with a new vim and vigour, 'No need to carry me now!'

They left the cottage and walked silently back to the graveyard in the gloom of first light. 'Quickly, lay me down in my bed,' he said, and then as she was helping him down into the coffin, he said, 'Lie with me!' and suddenly he grabbed her around the neck, pulling her down, and she struggled to free herself, and she shouted, 'I will not!'

He replied, 'You must and you shall!' and he forced her down with him into the coffin, for he was surprisingly strong, and then shut the lid down over them.

Now, if there was trouble before, that gave Mary a whole new pile of trouble, lying in the dark, her face pressed against the clammy skin of a corpse, his arms clasping her in a death-grip.

Time passed. And more time.

Mary waited and wished she'd left the stick where it was in the ground.

Mary had no concept of how many hours she lay in the dark, feeling as cold as the ice in January. She tried to calm herself and think ... what to do? The corpse was silent but retained its steely grip.

Well, after a long time, or quite possibly only a short time, she could not tell, the corpse began gently snoring, so Mary slowly tried pushing the coffin lid open, and then, slowly, she extricated herself from the embrace of the corpse and scrambled out of the grave. She closed the lid, piled the turves back on and hurried back to the village.

By now, it was the middle of the day, but she couldn't tell which day it was. When she arrived, she noticed how quiet it all was, not a soul about the place until she saw old Mrs Fitzpatrick, who said, 'Have you heard? The Flattery brothers have been murdered in their beds; their throats slit. Everyone is up there. You'd best go and see for yourself.'

So, she did, and sure enough, the whole village was there, and there was a right old commotion and a weeping and a wailing in a wake that was in full swing. Mary went to the sister of those brothers, took her aside and she said, 'Now, you might think I'm crazy for saying this, but I'm not, so hear me out.'

She told the sister that she might be able to bring the brothers back to life, and if she was successful, in return she would like the gift of the small field at the top of the hill. And the sister was willing to agree, of course, and so Mary went upstairs alone with the two corpses to pay her respects.

In the bedroom, she stuffed some of the oatmeal bread in between their cold lips and watched as the pale flesh suffused with blood and the eyes fluttered open, at which point she clapped her hands and she shouted, ''Tis a miracle!' And of course, it was.

What story she then told to everyone we'll never know, but I do know that not long after she went up to that field and dug for that gold, and found it, and then she went down to the churchyard, opened up that grave and hammered down the lid of the coffin with a hundred nails, then she covered it with the heaviest boulders she could carry, and picked up the blackthorn stick that was still lying there and delivered it back to the old man.

On being presented with the stick, the old man grinned, and said, 'Well, you have got the spirit – enough to be my wife!'

'I will not,' she said.

And the old man fixed her eyes with his, and said, 'You must and you shall!'

Mercy Bestowed

Dartmoor, Devon, England

Once upon a time on Dartmoor, there was a man and a woman who had twelve children. When their thirteenth was born, it put them into a panic, as there was so little money to feed and clothe them all. They were destitute and desperate and couldn't help but blame their situation on an uncharitable God in heaven.

One day, the husband was walking home through Hembury Woods, bemoaning his fate as a poor man. It was the dimpsy time, and in the twilight, he saw a luminous figure seemingly hovering on the trail ahead. As he drew closer, he saw an old man, radiant and glowing like an apparition but benevolent and unthreatening.

The apparition spoke to him kindly and gently, 'Fear not for your new-born son. I will be the guardian and I will ensure his happiness and contentment.'

Well, the husband knew it must be a revelation from a celestial and gave vent to his frustration, 'No! You are the one who lets the honest, hardworking poor starve and the rich good-for-nothings prosper.' And with that, the vision disappeared, and he continued on his way.

After another half a mile, he came to a track and out of the deepening gloom, a black carriage and black horses rolled up, and a man peered out. He was dressed all in black, wore a black, broad-brimmed hat, and a dark, richly embroidered cloak. His eyes were like red, glowing coals and his voice was like gravel. 'Rest assured, your worries are over, I will be the godfather of your child! He will be wealthy beyond measure and have plenty of influence and prestige.' He knew at once he was the Devil.

'I think not to entrust him to your corrosive care!' he blurted and watched as the carriage rumbled away and out of sight.

He hurried on for home and reached the top of Buckfast, and as he started down the hill towards the river, he saw an old woman, completely shrouded in rags, coming towards him up the lane. 'What next?' he asked himself, and somehow was not surprised to see her black, tattered rags and a cascade of silver hair gathered about her spindly waist. Her face was wrinkled and pale and when she spoke, he felt the air chilled around him. He knew she must be Death. 'I will be the godmother to your child. I will make him a healer. I will show him the herbs and potions of the open moor, woodland copses and the foreshore.'

He peered into her empty eye sockets and felt strangely calm. 'Well, as Death, you take from poor and rich alike when you claim their lives, and that seems fair to me. You alone recognise that all the power and prestige in this world means nothing when you cross that final border. I agree therefore, if anyone from the other realms is to be guardian for my boy, then let it be you.'

So there, at the top of Buckfast Hill, in the gathering gloom of dusk, they shook on it, and a bargain was made. She vanished as mysteriously as she'd appeared, and he quickened his pace home.

The years passed and Death was as good as her word. His son, who they had named Joseph, grew up to be strong and healthy and with a great interest in medicine. He quickly became skilled in the healing arts.

One day, Death appeared to him in a dream and gave him knowledge of a specific plant and said, 'When you are doing a healing, if I appear at the top of the bed, give them this medicine, if I appear at the bottom, let them go, for they belong to me.'

Well, his fame and reputation spread as all who employed his talents made unexpected recoveries. Word of his extraordinary capacities travelled to wherever there was sickness, and eventually brought him to the sickbed of the King.

This, of course, was going to either seal his reputation or destroy it, if he failed to cure this patient.

Just as he was about to administer his medicine, he caught sight of Death slowly materialising at the bottom of the bed. He panicked and immediately called to the servants to switch the bed around so the King's head could be nearer the open window. 'Quick, quick! The King needs fresh air!'

The servants moved so swiftly, the healer saw, that by the time Death had manifested, she was now at his head. He quickly applied his medicine and the King's fever broke and he revived.

That night, Death came visiting in a dream. Hovering above his bed, she extended a long white arm and placed a cold hand on his chest and said, 'Don't you ever do that again. Only I know when it is time for the crossing.'

Time passed and, of course, his reputation as a wondrous healer was secured and gave him the position of the King's physician. Eventually, he and the King's daughter fell in love.

For a while, for this thirteenth son of a penniless pauper, things could not be better. But, having climbed a mountain and enjoyed the view, the descent must follow. The King's daughter succumbed to the same ailment as her father and grew gravely ill, despite his healing administrations.

He could not prevent Death appearing one day at the bottom of her bed. Terrified, he quickly picked her up and placed her back down with her head at the bottom of the bed. Immediately, he fed her his potion and she revived. He had cheated death a second time and he turned fearfully to the spectral figure hovering in the room. This time, however, Death did nothing, but turned and quietly floated out the room. He waited for some recrimination from Death, but none came.

Time passed, the courtship continued and soon they were married, amid much rejoicing, feasting, dancing and singing. That night, as he gazed upon his bride as she slept with the moonlight dappled on her lovely face, he suddenly felt chill in the chamber. Suddenly, Death was there in her tattered shrouds, her face as usual obscured, and she was beckoning with one bony finger.

Trembling, he followed, not knowing if he was dreaming. She went down the stone staircase, out of the castle, through the cobbled streets until, finally, they came to an opening in the hillside. Death disappeared into the dark recess, and he followed, not without trepidation, wondering if this was to be his final descent. She led him down a long tunnel until it opened into a huge, cavernous chamber where he saw a glow of thousands upon thousands of candles, giving a buttery, golden light. Some were upright and bold, casting a fierce light, others just a dribble of wax and a flickering flame.

Death turned to him and said, 'These are the lives of all the people who still live on this earth.' As she said this, it seemed to him that new candles would appear here and there, while other areas would suddenly go dark.

Death led him through the chamber and stopped before one candle. Somehow, he knew it was his own life flame he was looking at, and its flame was tiny, flickering and spluttering.

He fell to his knees and said, 'Please, I beg you! Please show me mercy.'

A thin, wavering voice spoke from the shroud. 'Mercy, you want? I already showed you mercy. Mercy was given when I let you revive the King and warned you then. Mercy was given when I let you revive your sweetheart. Mercy was given when I let you have your night's embrace together. The time for mercy is over. Life is infinitely precious – precious beyond all measure – but it's up to me, Grandmother Death, to know the time and nature of departure, not you.'

And with that, one long, lithe, white arm reached from her coal-black shawl and pinched out the candle.

Black Annis

Buried under the concrete of a housing estate to the west of Leicester, in the Dane Hills, lies a cave containing the underworld stories of a terrifying witch-demon they called Black Annis. She was unnaturally tall, with a blue-grey face, just a few yellow, sharp teeth, and she ate people.

She was dressed in a tattered black nun's habit, which some say was from her time at the nunnery, from where she fell from grace a century before. It was said she'd dug out the cave where she dwelt with her long, sharp fingernails, and in her bitterness, haunted the Dane Hills between dusk and dawn looking for victims. She preferred the sweet flesh of children, if she could get it, but if she couldn't, she would live off the many sheep in the pastures, much to the farmers' consternation.

When people would hear the grinding of her teeth and her pig-like snuffling, they would hurry to fasten any windows they'd forgotten to close. Cottages were built with tiny windows, and babies were never left near them, wary of one of Annis' long arms reaching in to snatch their beloveds.

Once, there were three children whose misfortune was a stepmother who was as cruel as she was unkind. She was always giving them unpleasant or even dangerous tasks to get them out of the house or into trouble.

One day, she sent them out late in the day to collect firewood. As night descended, they feared for their lives, for in those times, the darkness contained terrors that could not be explained – things that lurked, waiting to do harm, especially to the young and innocent. Which is why loving parents called them in as the tide of darkness swept in.

So, here were three children, out for longer than they should be, trying to gather the firewood for their wicked stepmother, fearing her wrath and punishment if they didn't complete the task, and fearing, in particular, the prospect of meeting Black Annis, who only came out after dark.

Jimmy, the eldest, carried a 'seeing stone', which had a hole through which he kept looking to locate any evil roaming abroad. When they'd almost gathered enough sticks into bundles of faggots, his little sister Jenny said, 'Look through the stone, Jimmy.'

Looking through the hole in the stone, Jimmy saw the spectral figure of the demon-witch Annis staggering through the gloom of dusk towards them. 'She's coming! Run!' he shouted to the others, and they dropped their bundles and took to their heels as fast as it was possible in the deep dusk.

Fast they ran, but Annis was faster and would have caught them but for tripping over those bundles, and they heard her howling with pain. Bruised and bleeding, she picked herself up and, now full of rage, she pursued the hapless children, gaining on them with every step. She surely would have caught them, too, had it not been for their father who'd come out to search for the missing children.

Around the first village corner they ran, crying and screaming, with Annis stretching her arms out to grab the hair of the little girl trying to keep up with her brothers. And just as those long, claw-like fingernails tangled into the girl's hair, the big felling axe wielded by her father smacked into Annis' head and she let go.

She cried, 'Blood! Blood!' and went running off into the darkness and was never seen again in the Dane Hills.

It took a hundred years or more until the darkness of the Dane Hills felt safe to enjoy, unless of course, this story was told to keep the children from wandering too far from home.

See No Evil, Hear No Evil

Mayo, Ireland

In the west of County Mayo, in old Ireland, there was a sacred stone chapel where it was said that dreams crossed and tarried to gather the stories of the living. And sitting on the steps of this chapel, there was a blind man by the name of Tadgh, which means 'one who speaks poetry'. Here he would sit, plucking his harp and telling and singing the old stories of Ireland to whomever would stop and listen.

He was never short of an audience, for his tales of old history were always compelling, and his sweet voice and the music of the harp would draw in the priests and the paupers to learn of their ancestors. So, this bard was cared for by the community, who made sure he was warm and fed.

The story begins one evening, when there was no moon, and the darkness was deep and strange. Tadgh was playing his harp when he heard footsteps approaching. This, of course, was not unusual, but the hour was very late. A deep voice said, 'Tadgh, I am here at the bequest of my Lord, who is visiting this sacred ground. He requests your presence to tell the story of the Two Battles of Mag Tuired that tells how the Tuatha Dé Danaan took Ireland from the Fir Bolg, and the Fomorians.'

'I'd be glad to feed hungry ears,' said Tadgh, 'but alas I am blind and cannot make my own way.'

'I will escort you,' said the stranger. 'But let us hurry as his court eagerly awaits your harp and voice.'

He was guided for what seemed like an unquantifiable passage of time, and after a long or short time, entered through a heavy iron gate. Tadgh immediately discerned the murmuring of many voices and, as they approached, a sudden quiet before the booming voice of his host welcomed him to the gathering and thanked him for coming. 'We would be most honoured to hear this epic tale.'

'Forgive me,' said Tadgh, 'although I have a willing tongue ready to wag for your pleasure and delight, I fear this tale is too long for one single night.'

'Well then,' replied the Lord, 'we insist on your return until the saga is concluded.'

'May it be so,' said Tadgh and picked up his harp and began the tale.

The skill of his fingers on the strings brought forth the splash of oars, the wind in sails, the clash of sword on shield, the flight of a thousand arrows and the din of battle. The quality of listening was so intense that Tadgh was carried on a euphoric tide of telling.

At the end of the night, and before the dawn, the Lord cried, 'Stop! Enough for this night – return at the same hour tomorrow but tell no one of your visit to this assembly.'

He was taken back and he slept through the following day until the appointed hour of the night when the deep-voiced stranger escorted him to the iron gates, and to his seat again to continue the tale. For six nights it was the same, with Tadgh none the wiser as to whom he was telling.

His audience, however, was the best he'd ever had. They hung upon his every word and note and rose and fell with the fortunes of the protagonists, weeping deepest emotion as the chapters of the battle unfolded before them, and weeping at the demise of the Fomorians in the second battle.

But Tadgh's nightly disappearances began to be noticed by the priests in the temple and by the community, who were deprived of the sound of his harp in the daytime, finding him asleep instead. Curiosity became concern, until it was decided among the priests to find out where the bard was going every night.

Quietly, they lay in wait on the darkest of nights, and when the strange messenger arrived, followed them to the iron gate, the entrance to an old, forgotten cemetery. This was where the Fomorian King had been buried after the second Battle of Mag Tuired. They crossed themselves before crossing that threshold and, clutching crucifixes, they entered and saw Tadgh with his harp on his lap, sitting at the tomb of the fallen king, and gathered all around him were flickering lights, lanterns that nobody living could have lit.

The priests rushed forward in horror to rescue Tadgh, shouting his name, but he didn't seem to hear them. He was lost in the tale, and in his audience of flickering flames. 'Tadgh! You are playing for the dead!' remonstrated the priests.

'Nonsense!' said Tadgh. 'I am telling the story of the Two Battles of Mag Tuired, as I have been doing these last six nights, and you are interrupting the tale's end.'

The priests, however, argued no more and instead grabbed Tadgh and forcibly took him back to the chapel. There, they explained to him that he was substantiating those dead spirits with his tale, and they were growing in numbers and in stature. His magical art was giving them life force, and it put everyone in danger.

He submitted to the explanation and to the ritual processes to cleanse him of his transgressions with the Otherworld, and they made a plan to help Tadgh evade the seduction of the dead.

That night, Tadgh lay down, quiet and still, and when at midnight he heard footsteps approach, he began to pray, with the understanding that if he gave all his attention to prayer, he would be immune from abduction. He lay in the dark and while praying, he heard the familiar deep voice call out, 'Tadgh! Our master awaits the end of the tale.'

Tadgh resisted the temptation to respond and focused instead on his prayer. 'Where is the bard?' the voice was heard to say, and the footsteps came ever closer.

Tadgh held his breath.

'Ah!' said the voice, 'here is the harp. But where is the player?'

A heavy silence descended, and Tadgh felt the weight of it, but was resolved to give his attention only to his prayer. Finally, the voice said, 'Well, I see no bard. All I see is two ears – better than nothing, I'll take them to my Lord.'

Tadgh felt a wrenching pain as his ears were torn from his head, but somehow, he refrained from crying out and at last the footsteps retreated into the darkness.

In the morning, the priests found Tadgh with bloodied stumps where his ears would have been. They bandaged him and looked into his blind, opaque eyes to see a man who was no longer there, and who had gone quite mad.

Tadgh never told another story, and the dead never received the end of their tale. In this way, that which was freely given was no longer received, and that which was taken was never given back.

Except, of course, this story – which at least in the telling, connects the living to the dead and reminds us that the dead want to hear the stories too.

The Demon Huntsman

On the Torquay coastline there lies, beneath the earth, the remains of an old submerged forest. At rare intervals, severe storms expose the ancient, petrified stumps of the trees, affording a rare glimpse into the past. At these times, such an anachronism contributes to the widely held notion that the whole area is 'thick with a primeval force'.

Many and diverse are the legends and stories of sinister goings-on, both ashore and at sea. The geology records the events, as stories are recorded in the place names. This can be seen at 'Daddy's Hole', or 'Devil's Hole', which is a deep cleft in the rocks on the edge of the town, and which they say was caused by the following story.

Long ago, in a pleasant village close to the sea, there lived a sweet maiden, proud and pretty. She was desperately in love with a handsome young squire, who lived on the neighbouring estate, but her love was not requited, as he was already betrothed to another.

Thus, it was that the young maiden resorted to carry her aching, broken heart on long walks, and on one such occasion she was by the sea when she happened upon her rival, the woman he had pledged to marry. With a contemptuous stare and jealousy and hatred in her heart, she hurried past. She was so filled with dark and perfidious thoughts that before she realised where she was going, she found herself close by some rugged limestone rocks on the foreshore.

There she indulged her anguish and bitterness further, and when her cries of despair subsided, the silence and stillness of that late summer evening was suddenly broken by the sound of baying hounds. Upon turning around, she was confronted by the sight of a cloaked rider, approaching fast through the twilight on a huge black stallion. Behind them, trailed an angry dark cloud of spectral hounds, barking and snapping as they ran. As they drew close, the terrified maiden swooned to the ground.

Upon awakening, she was however, surprised to see a handsome young man bending over her, clearly concerned for her welfare. Still trembling from the memory of that apparition, she asked the young gallant if he had witnessed the scene containing the Demon Huntsman and his hellhounds. He replied that he'd seen nothing unusual and that he'd happened to be near at hand because he had been seeking solace and solitude by the sea to bewail his lost love. This rather drew the young maiden's interest and sympathy and before long, she found herself telling the kind and gentle young man of her own broken heart.

When she'd finished telling the sorry tale, he accompanied her back to her village and agreed to meet the next night.

The two of them met the next night, and for several more after that. It seemed he only wanted to meet during the hours of darkness, but as he had her affections, she thought nothing of it. The courtship was brief, but the bond between them was quickly, and fatefully, sealed.

Despite that, she still suffered bitterness and harboured vengeful thoughts. One night, her new lover said, 'This was most unfair and cruel. If I were to promise you your full and complete revenge, would you pledge yourself to me, forever?'

The maiden's jealousy was still hot inside her, and the young man's demeanour so frank and earnest, his eyes so beguiling, that she agreed to the bargain at once and she considered herself fortunate indeed to be pledged to one so handsome and apparently refined.

At length, he told her of a certain place by the sea, where he knew the young squire often arranged to meet with his bride-to-be. The next evening, with a mad desire for revenge stoked and fuelled by the young man consuming her heart, the jealous maiden stole softly through the twilight toward the meeting place. Upon encountering the two lovers clasped in each other's arms, she drew the dagger from her girdle and stabbed them both before they had the chance to protect themselves.

The dreadful deed was done, and as she stood above the murdered lovers, a frightful storm suddenly arose. Dark clouds roiled above and thunder rolled and lightning flashed, brightening the gathering gloom with vivid glare, illuminating the macabre scene.

The clamour of the storm was pierced by the sound of baying and a brilliant flash of lightning revealed that same rider approaching on the same black, swarthy steed. The dark cloud of dogs was at his heels and as they drew closer, the young maiden realised with increasing dread that the man approaching was none other than her newly betrothed lover. She turned and clambered desperately over the rocks to escape, but in vain, for her doom was at hand.

First, the hellhounds caught her and tore at her dress and the Demon Huntsman was heard to cry out triumphantly, 'At last, you are mine, forever!'

The storm increased in fury, the thunder boomed and the earth shook – down in the rocks a fiery abyss opened up and the Demon Huntsman, uttering a loud peal of mocking laughter, grasped his terrified prey and vanished into the hole, pursued by the spectral hounds.

The cleft in the rocks never closed, and though the maps now record it as 'Daddy's Hole', it really should be called the 'Devil's Hole' to remind us that hearts remain soft only by loving and being loved. A heart starved of love, hardens and cracks open, and that's how the Devil jumps in!

Seven

Tales from Betwixt and Between

Introduction

In the universe, there are things that are known, and things that are unknown, and in between them, there are doors.

William Blake

I've given these tales their own chapter because they are the uncategorisable sort of stories that both enchant and mystify and have a pinch of strangeness to tip them into the territory of the imaginal.

Stories are themselves liminal, in that they are both 'real' and imaginary and sit at a crossroads or junction between reality and illusion. They conjure up extraordinary events amid an everyday narrative and for that they command our attention.

Just like our forebears, we love to escape from the routines and harsh vicissitudes of everyday life. Many in my audiences have expressed a 'longing for the enchantment of the story world', which, from the perspective of a modern industrialised world, is a recognition that there is a certain medicine in visiting otherworldly or long-lost paradigms.

Like a real-world travel adventure, there are things to be gleaned and gained from journeying to other places, and the more 'other' they are, the more there is potential for non-ordinary states to be induced in the listener.

An interruption in the daily grind to climb into the time machine with the storyteller affords us respite from ordinary perceptions of people and places, and opens our eyes to different characters, landscapes and situations. At least, outwardly so, for in truth, the stories offer us allegories of our own lives, dressed up in otherworldliness but speaking back to us a commentary or insight into living differently or just living better.

Enjoy them for what they are – stories. Have faith that from the place of betwixt and between, you are in safe but stimulating hands.

Fox Fire

Once upon a time, there was a young malcontent, a young farmer who was always dreaming of another life. "Tis a man's sorry path to work hard and be poor,' he was often heard to say.

One night, after staying late at the market to drink in the tavern and bemoan his fate, he was on his way home, his trail through the woods illuminated by the dappled silver light of a full moon. As he was stumbling along, suddenly he saw ahead of him an unexpected apparition, stopping him in his tracks. Otherworldly, it seemed, and he drew back into the shadow of a large oak tree to observe the strange sight.

There was a fox standing in a shaft of moonlight, and in its mouth was something shining, like a bright crystal ball of silver. As if this wasn't enough of a mystery, he was even more astonished when he saw this ball float like a bubble up toward the moon, and then sink back down, right back into the jaws of the fox.

The farmer watched this happen repeatedly, and it dawned on him that the stories of foxes making the elixir of life at full moon must indeed be true, though nobody as far as he knew had ever seen it, finding only the strange residues of glowing things on the forest floor. He also knew that the stories foretold that anyone ingesting the fox fire, would imbue themselves with gifts of healing and insight and prophetic wisdom, and the veil between worlds would become as transparent as glass.

With this in his mind, and with the fortifying mead he'd drunk from the tavern, he lurched forward as the fox fire was floating down from the canopy. The fox jumped away in alarm at the sight of the burly young man emerging from behind the oak, and a bubble of silvery light came to rest in the farmer's hand. He stared into its luminous mystery. He was hypnotised. He saw it was like a silvery, swirling cloud, spinning around itself.

He would have been content to watch this strange magic for the rest of the night, but he remembered the old adage about the good fortune he would receive if it was swallowed. Not without some trepidation, he put it into his mouth and gulped it down whole.

It was ice cold, and he had to repeatedly swallow hard until he could feel it rested in his belly. At first, nothing happened, but from that time on, things changed for the young farmer. All of those prophecies were made manifest in the form of supernatural powers. His ability to heal the sick became widely known, and this earned him a comfortable living. He was consulted on hauntings and happenings and was able to intervene and settle any dispute by intercourse with the spirit world.

For a score of years this continued, until one summer evening, he was sitting with a goblet of wine and contemplating withdrawing from the burdens and responsibilities of life, when he dozed off in his chair. Suddenly, he was startled awake, coughing and spluttering, as if he'd been slapped on the back with some force.

The twilight had deepened all around him, but his eye caught a movement in the distance and he saw a fox trotting off toward the woods, and trailing behind the fox, was the silvery fox-fire ball. As the fox vanished into the trees, so did the fox fire, and the farmer had the sense that his mysterious gift had left him for good, taking all its capacities and qualities with it.

He sank back into his chair and fell into a deep contemplation. He remembered how he'd stumbled across it, all those years ago, and what good fortune it had brought him. He fell to wondering about its provenance and purpose. And after all these reflections, he was left with the same question – one that arrives to all of us in the latter years of our lives.

Did we make the most of it, while we had it?

Fishbones in the Sky

Aboriginal Australia

Wahn was a Crow, full of mischief, and Baripari the Cat was his friend and accomplice. Together, they devised a clever way to catch fish from the sea. They built a low wall of stones that would be covered by the incoming tide and would retain water when the tide ebbed. That way, any fish swimming into the saltwater lagoon at high tide would get caught behind the stones.

Wahn and Baripari were able to supply their people with plenty of fish to eat, much to the resentment of other tribes who were jealous of this successful harvest.

One day, on a particularly high tide, Balin, the leader of the Barramundi tribe of fish, was caught in the trap. He called out to the rival tribes and asked them to release him and his relatives. He was hoping they would set him free in exchange, but those people didn't. Instead, they took all the fish, and they dug shallow pits, made fires, cooked and ate them all. By the time Wahn and Baripari returned to the lagoon, there were just piles of fishbones everywhere.

Wahn was irritated by the loss of food, but he was more upset to find the big bones of Balin, a beloved and respected totem. 'Balin was my friend – I would never have dared to eat him,' said Wahn.

'What shall we do?' asked Baripari. 'It is our fault he is gone.'

Wahn thought for a while. 'Let us pay due respect to his memory. Let us make a burial ceremony. I'll gather his bones, and you fetch a hollow-stemmed tree.'

When Baripari returned, dragging the tree behind him, the two friends cut off the branches and then stuffed Balin's bones down the hollow stem, sealing the ends with mud.

All this had taken time, and it was now dark. 'Now what?' asked Baripari.

Wahn gazed up into the night sky. 'Look,' he pointed. 'There is the Milnguya River. Up there it is quiet and peaceful, far away from predators and the wicked ways of our rivals. Let us place the burial post on the riverbank there.'

Wahn and Baripari, assisted by their relatives, flew up to the sky-river and laid the post on the riverbank. There, they made ceremony for Balin, and afterwards, Baripari said, 'This is such a peaceful and pleasant place. I feel like I could stay here forever.'

'Me too,' replied Wahn. 'Let's light our campfires and rest a while.'

So, they did, and they are still there, and the smoke from those many campfires makes the shining mist we can see in the Milky Way (*Milnguya* or sky-river).

The Rope of Light

South Africa

In the hot, dry *veldt* of Southern Africa, where the people pray every year that the rains will come and grow the grass for their cattle, there was a young herdsman. Like all herdsmen, his pride and joy were his cattle, and he tended them well, ensuring that their udders were always full, and that there was a constant flow of milk for the village. More than any other cows, his were envied for their health and fertility.

The only aspect of his life that was unsatisfactory was that he did not find a wife. For whatever reason, no young woman had been attracted to him, and it wasn't for the want of trying that he remained alone, and was somewhat sad that he might spend the rest of his days alone. Despite this, he remained faithful to his herd, and was at least a good husband for them.

The story begins when, one day, his cows produced no milk. This was unusual for his cows, but not unusual for others. When the udders were dry the next day, he began to wonder what had caused it. After the third day, when no milk was forthcoming, he began to get seriously concerned.

In the days that followed, there was no more milk, and the herder began to attend in different ways to whatever might be causing the symptom. He spent every day watching them graze to see if they were eating anything unusual. But they weren't. He gave them medicinal herbs to no avail. It was strange that all the cows belonging to the other herders continued to produce milk.

The herder was beside himself with worry. 'What if they give no more milk? They will surely be sacrificed for meat, and I don't want to lose them – they are all I have!'

So, the herder went to find the medicine woman, the *Sangoma*, of the tribe. She lived just on the edge of the village in a ramshackle old hut by the stream. After making her an offering, the old woman took her bag of 'bones' and cast them to the ground. She studied them for a long time, and then she turned to the herder and said, 'You must attend to your cows at night, for whatever is taking the milk, is thieving by night.'

She gave the herder some herbs to keep him awake as he watched, and that night he stayed with his cows. All night he watched and waited, but there was nothing but the nocturnal serenade of crickets and distant yaps of the hyaenas. The next night, he followed his cows under the light of the crescent moon, and again saw no thief at work. Still his cows produced no milk, and he sat for a third night watching for anything unusual, anything to explain the dry udders.

In the early hours of the morning, he'd had enough, and was just turning on his heel to return home when he noticed a strange light high in the sky. He watched this light unfurl, like a rope, a silver rope of light hanging down from the darkness, all the way down to the ground. As if this wasn't strange enough, he then saw seven figures slithering down the rope – seven women.

He hid behind a bush and watched them move between his seven cows, and then each began milking the cows into their *calabash*. 'So, now I've found the thieves,' muttered the herder, but he was too entranced by them to intervene. He was enamoured by them, for they were beautiful, particularly one of them, who he found especially alluring.

One by one, they returned to the silver rope and began to climb up. As the seventh woman got up to go, the herder was filled with anguish that he might be missing his only chance and rushed out from behind his bush. He reached the rope just as the last woman was climbing up. He grabbed onto her leg and pleaded with her to stay. She looked down at him, and she said calmly, 'If you let go of my leg, I will answer you.'

So, the herder let go, and looked at her, anxious in his heart, waiting for her to speak. She looked into his eyes, scouting out his heart, and whatever it is that passes between the eyes of new young love took lodgings there. She said, 'Wait through another cycle of the moon, I will return to you,' and then he watched her climb up the silver rope until the darkness swallowed her up.

The days that followed were the slowest of days, as he suffered the torture of not knowing if he would see her again. The milk, however, returned to the udders of his cows and life returned to normal, except that the herder knew that something had gained purchase in his heart, and he was now restless and impatient for the moon to wax and wane through its cycle.

When the slender crescent of new moon finally rose, he was out on the *veldt*, watching eagerly for a sign. All through that night he waited, but there was no silver rope. The next night, he waited again, but again nobody appeared. Night after night, under the waxing moon, he was there, growing ever more anxious to see her again.

As the moon began to wane, he despaired, and began to wonder if it had simply been a dream, when suddenly he saw a pinprick of light in the sky, not starlight, but a light that rolled down from the sky, a rope of shimmering, silver light that hung suspended from high in the darkness and down to the ground. He held his breath for what seemed like an age, until he saw the rope twitch, like a snake, and looking up, he saw a figure descending, carrying a basket.

His heart was racing, and soon he could see that it was her. She was even more beautiful than he'd remembered, and he raced over and would have flung his arms around her, but she held up a hand and said, 'Wait! Before I agree to come and live with you and be your wife, you must make me a promise.'

'Anything!' he replied. 'Tell me what it is.'

'You see this basket I am carrying? I will bring it into the hut. You must promise never to look inside it. If you keep your promise, I will stay with you.'

'I promise,' said the herder.

He took her to where he lived, and they settled into a life together, and they were blessed by the elders and married with all the village ceremony. The following passage of time passed sweetly. Their love blossomed, and the herder had everything he wanted. He loved to hear her sing as she went about her work in the hut and in their garden. Often, he would return home in the evening to a song and a pot simmering over the fire. Every day, he gave thanks for his good fortune, for what the night had delivered to him.

But, as the weeks rolled into months, and the months rolled into years, a curiosity arose in the herder to know what was in her basket. For a while, he dismissed the thoughts, remembering his oath. But, like a weed in the garden getting cut back and growing back stronger, the desire to know developed into a deeper curiosity, which turned into obsessive fantasies about what the basket contained.

Finally, he convinced himself that there really could be no harm in just having a look, and if he did, she would never know anyway. At length, the decision to look had taken root, and one day when his wife was out gathering herbs, he lifted the lid of the basket – and whatever he had expected to find there, it certainly wasn't. Inside the basket was nothing ... it was empty. The herder shrugged, and although surprised, thought nothing more of it, and went off to tend to his cows.

It was early evening when he returned to the hut. This time there was no song. And no fire. And no pot simmering. Instead, his wife was sitting quietly outside the hut, with her basket at her feet. 'Is everything alright, my love?' asked the herder, suddenly anxious.

She looked at him then, and she simply said, 'You looked in my basket.'

'Yes,' said the herder. 'I am sorry. But there was nothing there!'

'Whether there was or there wasn't,' said his wife, 'you should not have looked in my basket.'

So saying, she left. She did not come back that night. Or any night thereafter. Presumably, she climbed the silver rope to return from whence she came.

We will never know. And nor will the herder, who spent the rest of his days regretting breaking his promise.

The Island of Bones

First Nations, America

A father told his son, 'Do not wander to the lake in the east, for there is only peril that awaits there.' As the boy grew, he explored the forests to the west of his village, but as his acquaintance deepened with the trails and trees, he grew ever more curious about what lay beyond what was known.

At length, he convinced himself that no harm could be done by simply looking at the lake, and fearing the wrath of his father, he waited until night had perched on the eyelids of his father and mother and stole silently out of the hut. By the light of the full moon, he walked softly eastwards.

As he strayed into the unfamiliar territory of the east, his apprehension grew and he was on the point of turning back when he saw the lake ahead, shimmering and glimmering in the moonlight. His curiosity got the better of him and soon he was standing at the lake shore and gazing out through the mist and silent water to an island of trees, a stone's throw away. The distance would have been a tempting one to swim by day, but the boy shivered with the night's cold and instead began throwing stones to see if he could throw as far as the island. The quiet night soon began to be disturbed by the plop and splash of stones breaking the stillness of the water.

He was entirely focused on this when he was startled by a soft voice behind him, which said, 'Let's see who can throw furthest.' The boy turned to look at a stranger, who was now standing on the lakeshore.

The moon had disappeared behind a cloud, and the boy could not quite make out the face of the man, but the voice was gentle, and he was always up for a game, so he said, 'What reward awaits the winner?'

'If you win, I'll take you to visit that secret island in my boat. There is treasure buried there.'

Well, that offer sealed the deal for this adventurous young lad, and so they began to throw. The stranger threw a stone far out into the lake, as far as the boy had ever thrown, but galvanised by the game and the prospect of a boat trip out to a secret island, he threw his stone with every ounce of strength he had at his disposal and managed to throw his stone beyond the stranger's.

'Well done!' said the stranger.

'So, where is your boat?' asked the boy, whereupon the stranger turned to the lake and began to chant in low tones while beckoning with both arms.

Almost immediately, appearing out of the silver mist were three swans towing a barge toward them. As soon as it breached the shore, the stranger stepped in and motioned the boy to follow. If there was a moment to turn back, this was it, and the boy paused. There was something all too compelling in this boat trip and, before he had even really decided, he was stepping into the boat, by which time it was too late as the barge pulled away towards the island.

The closer they got, the more apprehensive the boy felt, but within a few short minutes the barge breached the sand at the edge of the island and they were stepping out. As soon as they were embarked on the shore, the stranger struck the boy on the head and he fell to the ground, dizzied by the force of the blow and fainting into darkness.

When he came around, the stranger and the barge were gone, and he was alone on the island. This at least afforded him some relief, though his head was hurting, and he moved toward the trees to sit and consider his position.

As he was figuring out his options, an otherworldly voice muffled out beneath the ground next to him. 'If you would be kind enough to dig me out, I'd be very grateful.'

The boy was shocked and unnerved for there was no one about that he could see. 'I've had quite enough trouble for one night,' he said, 'and I'm not looking for any more.'

'There'll be more trouble for you if you don't,' said the weird voice from underground.

The boy considered for a moment, and quickly arrived at his conclusion. More trouble was distinctly unappealing and so he began to scrape in the sandy soil and soon saw something buried beneath. He scraped away more of the sand until he saw what lay in this shallow grave. As bone after bone emerged from its sandy chamber, he realised with horror that the voice belonged to a skeleton. 'Thank you, I am much obliged and for that kindness, I shall now help you. But first, please find my tobacco pouch, pipe and flint down the hole at the bottom of the nearest tree.'

The boy saw the hole and put his hand in to find all three items. 'Please put the tobacco in the pipe and light it and put the pipe in my mouth.'

The boy did exactly this and held it between the teeth and watched the skeleton puff on the pipe. 'Thank you,' said the skeleton. 'I'm tormented by the mice that nest in my bones, and smoke is the only thing that will move them.'

He puffed away, making clouds of smoke, while the boy stared, not daring to take his eyes off this strange scene of a smoking skeleton. When the tobacco was finished, the skeleton said, 'I expect you'll want to know how to escape this troubled island, and in particular, how to escape from the man that will return to hunt you. He wants to quench his thirst with your blood.'

'Yes, please help me,' said the boy, transfixed by every word.

'Listen carefully, you don't have long,' said the skeleton. 'He is fetching his dogs and will be back soon to hunt you for his dark sport. Before he comes, you must run quickly around this island to make many trails, leaving your tracks and scent everywhere. Make sure you touch every tree and then hide in the tallest tree you find. Then the dogs will not smell you.'

Thus, the boy ran hither and thither, doing exactly what had been asked, until he heard the baying of hounds across the lake. Terrified, he chose a big tree to climb, where he cowered in the canopy. For the rest of the night, he shivered and shook while the stranger and his dogs combed the island.

At the first sign of light, he heard the stranger say to his hounds, 'There is no sport tonight, my beloveds, let us return tomorrow.' The boy heard them slowly disappearing into the breaking dawn, and when all was quiet, and with the returning confidence of the morning sun, he clambered down the tree and went to where he'd left the skeleton, half wondering if this had all been a dream.

He was both shocked and relieved to find the skeleton exposed in the ground as before. The skeleton said, 'He will return this night, and you must be ready. Bury yourself deep in the sand where you think the boat will arrive. Take my pipe to make a breathing hole. After he has gone, and if the dogs haven't smelt you, make your way back across the water in his barge.'

'What about you?' said the boy. 'Shall I bury you again?'

'No,' said the skeleton. 'Let the wind and rain, moon and sun have their way with me. My bones want the weather, not the mice. Now give me the pipe again.'

All that day, the boy lit the pipe for the skeleton, and as the sun began its final descent, the skeleton gave him the last words of advice. 'Do not return to this island for the cycle of thirteen moons. When you return, bring me more tobacco.'

The boy promised, and then left by the light of the setting sun, down to the sandy shore to dig a hole for himself to hide and wait in the cold sand to learn of his fate, breathing the cold air through the skeleton's pipe.

He didn't have to wait too long before he heard the muffled baying of the hounds. He held his breath. The noise abated and he sensed his chance had come. He struggled out of his sandy tomb with the hunt in the far distance. Thankfully, the barge and swans were close by, and he quickly boarded. To his utter relief, the swans began paddling away, back towards the land he had left.

When ashore, he ran and didn't stop running until he was home. There, he suffered the recriminations of his father but said nothing of his strange adventure. He didn't venture east again, until the night of the thirteenth full moon arrived.

With fresh tobacco in his bag and the full moon lighting the way, he returned to the lakeshore to find the barge waiting for him. He was soon treading through the soft sand on the island where he again lit the pipe for the skeleton to clear away the mice and sat while they smoked and talked through the night. At length, the boy asked, 'Is there something more I can do for you? You did, after all, save my life. Shall I carry you back across the water and lay you to rest in my village?'

'You are most considerate,' said the skeleton, 'but I am content here, as long as you can come every thirteenth moon to smoke my pipe with me and move those pesky mice along, I'll be just fine. It won't take too long for the weather to do its work on me and there'll come a time when you'll not find me, and you won't need to visit.'

And so it was that every thirteenth moon, the boy came with fresh tobacco and sat with the skeleton a while, until time had worked its old magic and the bones slowly faded away. The boy had grown by now into an old man, and when he sensed his time had come, he left his village for the last time and ventured east, crossed the lake, put the pipe and tobacco in the hole by the tree, and lay down for his final rest in exactly the same spot where he'd found the skeleton.

The Legend of Lussi

Once, when the world was very young, and everything was bountiful, the first woman, Lussi, was created from the soil at the same time as Adam. They had many children together, and she was as strong and wilful as he was, and often they argued and fought. One day, God visited them in the Garden of Eden, but Lussi hid her children because they had been playing in the mud and she did not have time to wash them. She did not want them to be seen in their dirty, dishevelled state in case it incurred the displeasure of God.

When God asked to see them, she persistently refused to present them. This angered God, and he banished them from the Garden, to live in the underworld for eternity. There, Lussi's many children birthed and brought forth the first demons.

Every year in December, when the nights were longest and darkest, Lussi would emerge from beneath the earth, and she was always furious. She would ride across the sky on her broom, or sometimes a horse, and would terrify mortals if they were abroad at night, dispensing death and pestilence and screaming down the chimneys, ordering people to refrain from their work of baking and brewing.

However, on the nights following mid-December, she would encourage everyone to work hard to get ready for the Christmas period, and there was so much to be done. If anyone incurred her wrath during this time, she would cause injury and harm, but if the people indulged her demands, she gave the children gifts.

These days, in those northern countries, they still remember her and celebrate the dark times of the year with much industry and gift-giving.

The Flowers Gave Us Sleep

India

In the very olden days, when Time itself was new to the world, the first people delighted in the rich abundance of the Earth's delights. In fact, their delight and endless curiosity was continuous – so much so that they didn't sleep. There was always something to do, work to be done, something new to see and, of course, when the work was finished, there was always the prospect of a game, some mischief, or a song to sing ...

The Creator god was Nanga Baiga, and she saw that people were never resting, that no slumber came to them, as it did to the animals and birds. She also saw that the people were sometimes irritable and grumpy with each other and did not perform their tasks to the best of their ability. Nanga was wise enough to know that every living thing would benefit from rest and recuperation and the very best recipe was a good night's sleep. But how could this be brought about?

She turned the matter over and over in her mind but could not figure it out. She knew it wouldn't work to simply instruct the people to lie down in the dark, least of all those playful children.

So, Nanga Baiga herself went to sleep that night because she knew that the answer might come in the form of a dream. The next morning, she awoke with fresh inspiration. She brewed a special potion and she delicately inserted it into the wild lavender blooms, so that when the breeze blew, it would carry the fragrance and the potion into the air and into the eyes of the people, causing them to fall into a restful sleep. Nanga Baiga watched the potion work its magic beautifully, and at last the nights were spared from the noisy chatter and activity of the people.

What's more, the people were waking up refreshed and with more energy and clarity of perception and, most intriguingly of all, some of them were waking up with stories of their dreams, which they told to each other.

But Nanga Baiga soon observed the effect was temporary, and only lasted as long as the lavender was in bloom. She knew then that the secret was to inject different flowers that bloomed in different seasons throughout the year. So, she looked at all sorts of flowering plants to see which would work best at different times of year. In the end, she chose the following flowers:

January – gorse
February – holy basil
March – magnolia
April – California poppy
May – jasmine
June – St John's wort
July – elecampane
August – valerian
September – chamomile
October – ginseng
November – aconite
December – ashwaganda

And these flowers have been influencing our dreams ever since!

Dancing Demons

*Source Unknown (I Heard
it Around a WildWise Campfire)*

Once upon a time, in a cottage in the vast forest, lived twin brothers who had been born as hunchbacks. To all the world, they were as like as like to each other; nobody could tell them apart, like proverbial peas in a pod, though they were as different in disposition as the Devil and the deep blue sea.

One was called Ivor and the other Igor, and they were as contrasted in character as goodness and greed. Ivor was happy-go-lucky, easy-going and contented. Igor's nature, however, was as contrary as the snow in summer. Anything Ivor wanted to do, Igor would insist upon doing the opposite. Agreement was quite simply not in his nature, whereas argument and conflict were. The days were filled with the sound of his wrangling and quarrelling. It was anything but a peaceful life for Ivor, who was at his wits' end in search of a quiet life.

The story begins on Midsummer's Day when Ivor went into the forest to collect firewood. By late afternoon, in the warm sunshine, he'd grown tired. He'd been kept up late the previous night by an argument with his brother about whose turn it was to blow the candle out and so, feeling sleepy, he stopped to rest underneath a gnarled old oak tree, twisted with age. The mossy roots jutted up from the forest floor and made for a comfy armchair, and soon Ivor was fast asleep. He slept and he slept until he was suddenly awoken by the distant sound of manic laughter.

It was now dark; he'd overslept and thought he'd been dreaming. But as he peered into the forest darkness, there were more strange sounds, and what's more, they were now all around him and were moving closer. This was no dream, and he grew more and more afraid as the sounds of slobbering and slavering beasts grew louder.

He froze in fear when he suddenly saw a pair of little yellow eyes open right in front of him. He could just make out in the darkness that it was a small creature, no bigger than a rabbit, with leathery skin, hooves and horns upon its head, boggle-eyed, with bat-like little wings. And then there was another one, and another one, smaller ones and bigger ones, two-legged ones and four-legged ones. There were fatter ones, thinner ones, crooked ones and they were all twisting and turning, writhing and wriggling in strange movements.

Then, quite suddenly, they all stopped, and they all looked … and then they were all pointing at Ivor and laughing and shrieking. 'Euuugh! Look at it! It's disgusting! Ugly creature!'

Ivor was frozen to the spot and didn't know where to look, but then the first gremlin grinned and pointed at him with a bony finger. 'Let's see if it can dance!' it said.

'Yes! Make it dance!' said the others, and cackled with dark laughter, and they began to chant:

'Make it dance! Make it dance!
Its life is spared if it takes its chance!'

And they all rushed at the terrified Ivor and grabbed him with cold, clammy claws and bony fingers, hauling him to his feet and poking him and prodding him, chanting and urging him on until Ivor, fearing for his life, began hopping about with all the gremlins who, the more he hopped about, the more they hooted and squealed with delight.

Ivor was, in fact, a very good dancer, and soon he was shimmying and pirouetting on the forest floor. He danced like a demon and the gremlins loved it so much they would not let him stop, and for a long time they danced, until Ivor could bear it no longer and sat on the floor and begged them to let him go.

They said, 'If we let you go, you must come tomorrow, and to ensure that you do, we want something from you! We will keep it till you come back! Yes! We want a deposit!' At this, they began to grasp and paw at him. 'Give us something! Give us something! Give us something!' they chanted.

'What do you want?' said a terrified Ivor. 'My axe?'

'No!'

'My hat?'

'No!'

'My boots?'

'No!'

'What then?'

'We want … the lump on your back!!!'

And before he knew it, they'd swarmed all over his hunchback, and he swatted and slapped at them, and then, when they'd dropped off his back, he stood up and, wonder of wonders, he felt himself standing upright! He'd never before stood tall like this. He felt his back where his hunch should have been and was astonished to find it was no longer there.

The demons laughed and said, 'Now we've got it! You must return, if you want it back! And gold pieces shall be your reward, for you can dance like us!' And then, as suddenly as they'd appeared, they disappeared, vanishing into the darkness and silence of the night, evaporating like a strange dream.

Ivor scrambled home. By the time he'd got back, he was indeed wondering if it had been a dream. But there was no denying he was still standing upright.

And it did not escape Igor's attention in the morning. 'What happened to you? Where were you, and where is your hunch?'

When Igor heard Ivor's story and when Ivor told him that he would not be returning to those dark denizens of the deep forest for all the gold in China, Igor said, 'You idiot! It's well known that gremlins hoard gold! You numbskull! Tell me where it was! I'll go tomorrow and I'll fill my boots with gold from those gruesome goblins!'

That evening, he made his way down the same forest trail, following Ivor's directions until he found the twisted old oak. He settled down to wait, and he waited impatiently as the twilight rolled in and around him, and eventually he too fell fast asleep.

He was suddenly awoken by the distant sound of manic laughter. It was dark, and strange sounds were all around him and moving closer. It was just as Ivor had described, but even so, Igor was terrified as the gremlins closed in. He froze in fear as he suddenly saw a pair of little yellow eyes open right in front of him. And another pair, and then another pair. Like ghostly lights all being turned on, he was suddenly surrounded, and one of them said, 'You came back!' And then there was shrieking and giggling and then the chanting began:

'Make it dance! Make it dance!
Gold it has if it takes its chance!'

And they rushed over to Igor and grabbed him with cold, clammy claws and bony fingers, hauling him up and poking him and prodding him, urging him on until Igor, fearing for his life, joined the dance, and he was soon hopping about with all the gremlins hooting and squealing with delight about his feet.

Now Igor had never been a good dancer, but the silent horror show continued, even though Igor could only stumble and stomp clumsily. At last, when it was finally over, one of the demons clapped his clammy hands together and said, 'Now, we will give you back what we took last night,' and before you could say 'Beelzebub', the gremlins had swarmed all over Igor's back, and as he swatted and slapped at his back to get them off, he felt a great weight descend between his shoulders.

'Here is your hunch back!' they shouted with glee. 'But no gold for a fellow that has forgotten how to dance!'

And they slithered away. They melted into the blackness of the night, slipping away like shadows, and Igor, like a fool, followed them, stumbling and shouting after them 'Where's my gold?'

He followed them so far into that forest that he was soon lost forever, and even though Ivor searched for him, he never did return. So, Ivor was left to live out his days without his troublesome brother, and without any of that gold, although at least he enjoyed some golden years in peace and quiet.

As for Igor, well, I often wonder what became of him. Perhaps he's still stumbling about in the dark, looking for gold?

And, lest you ever meet those little gremlins, just you make sure you can dance like a demon!

Swan Lights

When the world was young, all the birds and animals spoke freely to each other, and the early people would hear them boasting to each other about who was fastest or strongest or the most beautiful or clever. Some say this is how people learned to do the same, and why the world is full of competition and contest.

In the north countries, the winters are long and the snow piles upon snow, there were two flocks of swans who were arguing about who would be first to reach their summer feeding and breeding grounds to the north. It was spring, and they were readying themselves for the long journey.

After much wrangling and gesturing and posturing, the lead swan of the larger flock said, 'There is only one way to settle this matter. There must be a race. We will leave at dawn tomorrow!'

All agreed, and the next morning they were stretching themselves before the sun was up and taunting the rival flock with more boasts and bravado. 'Don't keep us waiting at the other end,' said one flock to the other. 'We'll have eaten all the best food before you get there!'

'Don't worry about that,' said their rivals. 'We'll beat you using only one of our wings – that's how easy it will be to win this race!'

So, when the sun eclipsed the eastern horizon, there was a huge flurry of wings and a scampering through the reeds at the lake edge, as swan after swan scrambled into the dawn sky. It was like a snowstorm moving up and out to the north.

I wish I could say it was a close race, but that would not represent the truth, for the larger flock soon had the edge and began to stretch their lead, leaving their rivals further and further behind. By the end of the day, they'd landed in a perfect feeding ground, and immediately began to gloat in their victory.

I suppose it was pride that, when the other flock finally appeared, kept them flying past them. Perhaps having boasted so much, they were ashamed to come down, or perhaps they decided upon a new game of who could fly furthest instead of fastest. We'll never know, but whatever it was, they flew on and kept going through the night and, despite their weariness, the next day too.

By the end of the next day, they were far beyond the northern country and into the farthest bone-freezing reaches of the world. At a certain point, it became so cold that the birds were frozen fast in the sky, which is where they still are today. But every so often they will attempt to fly, and with a great effort there is a rustling of wings. We know this, because light will be reflected off those fluttering feathers of white, and appear in the sky as the northern lights, or Aurora Borealis, as it has come to be known.

The Firefox

Finland

A long, long time ago, before the first before, there was a great forest called Midgard, in which lived an Arctic fox called Tulikettu, whose fur was as black as night. Tulikettu was cunning and sly, and loved to play tricks on the other animals of the forest. For that reason, he did not have many friends. His best trick was to brush his tail against the ground while running fast, and this would produce sparks, and sometimes this would set the grass alight. No other animal could do this, and Tulikettu enjoyed this magic trick.

One day, Tulikettu was wandering through the forest and he came across some rabbits and overheard them making fun of his unusual black fur. This infuriated him, so he sprinted past them, sweeping his tail so that the sparks flew and the grass caught alight. The rabbits were terrified and ran off into the safety of the forest to escape the fire.

This was not the first time that Tulikettu had caused such mischief, and the old *Landvættir*, or land spirit, who resided in the forest lake, summoned Tulikettu and scolded him for his constant misdemeanours, and banished him from Midgard to the ice-lands of trolls and giants, called Jotunheim. There, Tulikettu dwelt in resentment, constantly fleeing from the fierce trolls and giants, and because this land lay under a thick blanket of snow, his coat slowly turned from black to white, which is still the colour of Arctic foxes today.

One night, when it was bitterly cold, Tulikettu came across two travellers, warming themselves by a small fire. These were no ordinary men, as their appearance suggested otherwise. Tulikettu took note of the sly, cunning demeanour of one and the huge hammer in the possession of the other one.

Suddenly, over the horizon, a huge giant could be seen approaching, and Tulikettu knew this spelled trouble for these two travellers. He now knew what it meant to feel fear, and the years of suffering had tempered his mischief. He felt sorry for the two men because he knew they did not have the legs to outrun the oncoming giant. So, he waited until the giant got closer and then dashed out, sweeping his tail and sending up such a shower of sparks, that a whirl of fireballs lit up the night and stopped the giant in his tracks.

While the sky was ablaze, a revelation appeared above them in the form of a shimmering, multicoloured bridge, and immediately the travellers saw the path to it illuminated and raced along it. This bridge, known to the gods of Asgard, who used it to move between realms, was called the Bifrost bridge, and as soon as the travellers reached it, they turned and thanked Tulikettu. They made Tulikettu a sweet home at the base of the bridge and charged him with a sacred task. This was to guide those that are lost, by making sparks and fire in the sky, so they could find their way home.

Tulikettu has obliged ever since, and in gratitude, the people call these wondrous lights, *Revontulet*, meaning 'fox fires'. When you are lucky enough to behold the aurora borealis, remember Tulikettu!

Acknowledgements

In one sense, this book didn't take long to write, even though it was a couple of years after it was commissioned that I handed in the manuscript. Thanks to the forbearance of my commissioning editor, Nicola Guy, I was given leave to attend to an illness that parked the project for one year.

However, in another sense it has, of course, taken a very long time to write, because I've had to gain 'skin in the game' as a storyteller, practising, perfecting and refining this mysterious craft, and evolving myself in the role over the last twenty-five years. I still consider myself an apprentice, and long may that servitude continue.

So of course, I owe a debt of gratitude to the countless storytellers I've had the privilege to know and learn from. These include Ben Haggerty, Jan Blake, Hugh Lupton, Martin Shaw and Ashley Ramsden, to name but a few of the shining lights in the world of performance storytellers. But I also want to single out the much more 'local' hero who is Clive Fairweather, who taught me so much, without knowing it, about how to tell a good story really well.

My own students in my storytelling classes are also deserving of acknowledgement for the stealthy way they have inspired and informed my journey. There are too many to mention.

Yet again I must thank my beloved wife, Rebeh for her faith and support at a time when our home is a constant riot of small children's needs.

And, of course, to those who went before, who kept the tradition alive and on whose shoulders I and all storytellers today are standing. A deep bow to the tradition bearers.

A blessing on the tellers, the tales and those who are willing to listen.